"You Shouldn't Have To Lose Everything."

"And you're here to fix that?"

"Yes." Flashing on her reaction every other time he'd tried to offer his assistance, Gabriel thought it wise to add, "If you'll let me."

"I see. Well, here's your answer." Straightening, Mallory swiveled to face him, her eyes dark with something he couldn't identify—and anger so blatant a blind man couldn't have missed it. "Go to hell."

"What is your problem?" Gabriel demanded.

"You!" she shot back. "You arrogant, self-satisfied jerk!" Sucking in a breath, she yanked her arm free. "I don't want your pity or your charity. And I am not, nor will I ever be, some wrong you need to right!"

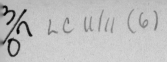

Dear Reader,

I knew early on what I wanted from life. A horse. From a tender age it was my only desire, and I hounded my parents relentlessly until I achieved my goal. A trio of beautiful animals and thousands of hours of joy and hard work later, I'd found my true calling. I was born to be a horse trainer.

Over the years my folks had reluctantly accepted I had no interest in dolls or dress up, ballet or piano, tennis or golf. They'd trudged through acres of sawdust, hauled me and my steeds a jillion miles, spent a small fortune on boots and bridles. But forgo a higher education for horses? Oh-kay. Of course, adult choices carry adult responsibilities, so I would have to start supporting myself…. And that's how I wound up going to college and becoming a writer.

Society princess Mallory Morgan is hit with her own real-world wake-up call when her scandal-plagued father decamps with the family fortune. Only, she has no safety net. Her very survival and what's left of her pride depend on her learning to stand on her own and take care of herself.

The only fly in the ointment is Gabriel Steele. The security magnate is dynamic, strong willed and accustomed to being obeyed. So when he decides it's his job to take care of Mallory, sparks fly—and the rules go out the window.

I hope you enjoy their story.

Caroline

CAROLINE CROSS

TAME ME

Published by Silhouette Books

America's Publisher of Contemporary Romance

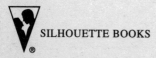 **SILHOUETTE BOOKS**
®

ISBN-13: 978-0-373-76773-1
ISBN-10:   0-373-76773-0

TAME ME

Visit Silhouette Books at www.eHarlequin.com

Printed in U.S.A.

Books by Caroline Cross

Silhouette Desire

Cinderella's Tycoon #1238
The Rancher and the Nanny #1298
Husband—or Enemy? #1330
The Sheikh Takes a Bride #1424
Sleeping Beauty's Billionaire #1489
*Trust Me #1694
*Tempt Me #1706
*Tame Me #1773

*Men of Steele

CAROLINE CROSS

Bestselling author Caroline Cross, winner of numerous awards, including the respected RITA® Award from Romance Writers of America, hopes that her books bring others a little of the pleasure she feels when she reads her own favorite authors.

Born and raised in the Pacific Northwest, she shares her life with her husband, two terrific daughters, a hundred-pound lapdog named Maddy and a circle of fabulous friends.

This book is dedicated with love to four terrific women I'm lucky to call my friends—

To Susan Andersen, who makes me a better writer in every way and who—thankfully—always knows what my characters think even when I don't have a clue.

To Barbara McCauley, whose optimism and generous spirit are a constant inspiration.

To Melinda McRae, who not only listens, but knows all sorts of unexpected things.

And to Kris Nelson, my long-lost sister…finally found.

One

Once upon a time when she'd still had a life, Mallory Morgan would've described Gabriel Steele as tall, dark and delicious.

That was before he'd cost her everything. Now, as she opened her flimsy apartment door and found him parked in the dingy hallway outside, the words that came to mind were hard, heartless and not-to-be-trusted.

"Mallory." As always his voice was quiet but commanding, the perfect match to his lean, powerful body and reserved green eyes.

"What do you want, Gabriel?"

"We need to talk."

"Do we?" To her relief she sounded calm and in

control, something that had eluded her earlier that day
when a chance meeting between them at Annabelle's,
one of Denver's trendier restaurants, had resulted in her
behaving badly—and paying a price she could ill
afford. "Gosh, let me think." Tipping her head to one
side, she pretended to consider for all of two seconds,
then straightened. "No."

With a flick of her wrist, she sent the door swinging
shut. It would just be too bad if it smacked him in his
autocratic chin.

He didn't so much as blink. Probably because the
cheap panel moved barely an inch before bumping against
his big booted foot. "Look, I get that you're angry—"

Her free hand tightened on the scarlet satin of the
robe that she'd thrown on over her bra and jeans at his
unexpected knock, bunching the thin, slippery fabric at
her throat. "What was your first clue? When I crossed
out your reservation and refused to seat you even
though the dining room was half-empty? Or when I quit
my job rather than apologize?"

"Don't be insulting. I caught on with your pig at the
trough comment."

"Then I believe we're done. Because I've certainly
got nothing more to say."

A grim smile touched his lips. "You don't want to
talk? Fine. You can listen then." Like the poster boy for
overbearing men, he slapped his palm against the wood
and pushed.

Instinctively she started to push back, only to check
herself as she realized he was already widening the

gap between jamb and door as if she didn't exist. Deciding she'd be a fool to engage in another battle she was sure to lose, she abruptly changed tactics.

"Well, since you insist…" Letting go of the doorknob, she gave a nonchalant shrug and took a giant step back. "By all means, come in."

To his credit, he didn't gloat. But it wasn't much consolation when the instant he crossed the threshold and the door shut behind him, she realized she'd miscalculated once again. No matter how big a hit her dignity had taken, she should have kicked, cried, screamed—done whatever she could to keep him out.

Because with Gabriel in it, her already minuscule studio apartment seemed to shrink. He not only took up all the available space, but also all of the air, making her feel small, breathless and far too…aware. Of his height, his power, his body heat. Of the jolt she felt when he looked at her.

It was hard to believe she'd once thought nothing of flirting shamelessly with this man. Not that it had meant anything—and not just because she'd had a carefully crafted reputation as a frivolous party girl to maintain. But because, her own shortcomings aside, she'd known early on that *he* was far too formidable for any involvement beyond a little lighthearted fun.

Still, whenever they'd bumped into each other at one or another of the Denver A-list's glittering soirees, she'd delighted in the subtle sizzle of mutual awareness that would envelop them, the way the air seemed to heat just a little with their proximity.

Inevitably, they'd wind up dancing, and she'd delight in leaning in close, in whispering outrageous suggestions in his ear, in watching the dangerous smile that would tug at his mouth when she trailed a fingertip along his jaw. The only thing better had been the proprietary way his hand would tighten on her waist when she rubbed her thigh against his as they circled the floor. That, and the amused glint of warning that would spark in his eyes, igniting a sharp little thrill she'd feel down to her toes.

All part of that other life, she reminded herself sharply. The one before Gabriel and his bedamned Steele Security had gone after her father and she'd lost her home, her friends, the last of her illusions and most of her self-respect.

Not to mention a fortune so large that up until it disappeared, her most pressing concerns had been along the lines of whether she should spend the weekend shopping in Paris or skiing in Gstaad.

It already seemed like a hundred years ago. And a distinct contrast to now, when she was already sick with worry about whether she'd be able to find another job that would allow her to both eat and keep a roof over her head.

That, however, was nobody's business but her own. Sure, Gabriel could barge in here, looking like a fallen Armani angel with his inky, razor-cut hair, beautifully tailored clothes and calf-length black leather coat, displaying the style she'd once jokingly dubbed "elegant badass." He could disturb her peace and stir up memories of a life she'd spent the past months trying to put behind her.

But he couldn't touch the core of her. She'd had years to perfect her defenses, to learn how to keep people in general at arm's length—and males in particular off balance.

The realization calmed her, allowed her to steady her bottom lip, which, infuriatingly, was threatening to quiver. Quietly blowing out a breath, she released her grip on her robe, knowing full well the effectiveness of a little insouciant sexuality as she reached up with both hands, gathered the long, unruly mass of her hair and tossed it behind her back.

"So?" She crossed her arms beneath her breasts, doing her best to look bored. "Are you just going to stand there? I thought there was something you simply had to say to me."

"Yeah. So did I." His expression gave nothing away as his gaze flicked from her eyes to her throat to the creamy V of her exposed cleavage before settling squarely back on her face. "I was wrong."

"You? Wrong?" She waited a beat, then smiled insincerely. "Surely not."

He didn't smile back. "I'd rather hear you talk. Why don't you tell me what the hell you're playing at, Mallory?"

"Excuse me?"

"I realize the past months must've been tough, but—"

"Tough?" Her voice started to climb; she wrestled

it back down. "Please." She flicked her fingers dismissively. "I was a debutante, and everyone knows that once you've learned how to waltz in high heels and make a perfect curtsy, you can handle anything. Having my home foreclosed on, my belongings auctioned off, my car repossessed, the family name dragged through the dirt by the press? No sweat. Learning the city bus routes, now, that's been a real challenge—"

"Don't," he said flatly. "I'm not trying to downplay the seriousness of the situation, and you know it. There's no excuse for what Cal did, ripping off the Morgan Creek investors, then bolting the way he did. But that doesn't explain what you're doing working at Annabelle's—"

"Formerly working at Annabelle's, thanks to you," she murmured, ignoring his reference to her father.

"—or living here, like this." He made a dismissive gesture that encompassed the kitchen with its single scarred counter and old hot plate as well as her living room-bedroom, where the nicest thing in the space was the pair of mismatched TV trays she'd lugged home from the Goodwill nine blocks away.

"I know, isn't it ridiculous? Just because I have limited funds, no job experience and a woeful lack of references, employers and landlords seem reluctant to take me on. Who would've figured?"

This time the jab hit home and that sensual mouth tightened, if only for an instant. "The last time I checked," he said evenly, "you had a trust fund that the courts and the banks couldn't touch."

"Ah, yes, my trust fund." Knowing she was on dangerous ground, she made a moue of regret—and shrugged, making no effort to stop the robe as it slid dangerously low on her shoulders. "The sad truth is, between travel and partying and my inordinate fondness for Jimmy Choos, Dom Pérignon and silk lingerie…it's gone."

"Are you serious?" He stared hard at her, clearly not certain whether to believe her or not.

She looked steadily back. "As a heart attack."

"And…this?" With a twirl of one long forefinger he indicated the shabby little room with its Texas-shaped water stain on the wall between the two narrow windows.

Before she could stop herself, she raised her chin a notch. "The best I can do."

He went utterly still, his impossibly green eyes seeming to spear right through her as he appeared to weigh her words. Then he uttered a single searing expletive and turned away, his coat billowing out as he paced three strides into her living room before running out of space.

"Get your things together," he commanded, his back still to her. "Whatever you'll need for tonight. I'll send someone for the rest tomorrow."

He couldn't have surprised her more if he'd fallen to the floor and declared he couldn't live without her. "What?"

He pivoted. "I said, pack a bag. You're not spending another night here."

Okay. This had to be a dream. She might feel wide-awake, but the truth was she'd fallen asleep on the lumpy little pullout sofa and everything that seemed so real—the chill of the worn linoleum against her bare feet, the faint, heady scent of Gabriel's aftershave, the jump of nerves in her stomach that his presence always provoked—was just a product of her imagination.

She cocked her head, wondering what would happen next. "And where, exactly, am I supposed to go?"

"My place."

Wrong again—definitely *not* a dream. Because no matter how wild and crazy her subconscious got, no matter how alone or desperate or frightened she felt, she would never consider moving in with him a solution to her problems.

It would be like agreeing to share a cage with a tiger.

Fascinating for maybe half a second. Totally terrifying after that.

So why, just for a moment, did she want more than anything in the world to take him up on his offer? Why did she want to close her eyes and step into the hard circle of his arms and say, yes, Gabriel, please take care of me?

Habit, she told herself angrily. Twenty-eight years of careless living, of always taking the easy path, of giving away her power and allowing others to dictate her fate.

Something she'd sworn on the day she'd been evicted from the estate that had been in her family for ninety years she'd never let happen again. A vow she refused to forsake, no matter how many jobs she lost or how many meals she had to skip to make ends meet or how long she had to live in a place like this.

If that meant thwarting Gabriel, who was, after all, responsible for lighting the fuse that had resulted in her life being blown up, it was simply an added bonus.

"Thanks so much," she said with patent insincerity, "but I'll pass."

She'd always considered him astute—on several occasions more than she might've wished—and he didn't disappoint her now. "You don't want to come home with me? Fine. Pick a hotel. You can stay there until I arrange something else."

She thought about her last experience at a hotel and shuddered. Still, she couldn't deny she was curious. "You'd do that? Put me up somewhere at your expense? Even if I tell you I'm not about to forget your part in everything that's happened?"

"Yes."

"Even though no matter how nice you pretend to be, I'm not going to sleep with you?"

"Yes, again—and I don't recall asking you to."

"Then why? What's in it for you?"

He shrugged, broad shoulders moving easily beneath the supple leather of his coat. "Peace of mind. It doesn't take an expert to know this place isn't safe. The building entrances aren't secure, there's no dead bolt on your door and I'd bet a year's profit an anemic five-year-old with a toothpick could jimmy your windows. Factor in that this is one tough neighborhood, which you're about as equipped to handle as a kitten dropped into a kennel of pit bulls, and there's no way I'm letting you stay here."

If it had been anybody else, she'd have considered

that last statement the height of bravado. But not Gabriel. In her experience, he said what he meant, then followed through.

Too bad that nobody—not even him—always got their way. "That's not up to you," she said flatly. "It's up to me. And I'm not going anywhere."

"Mallory." He spoke in the ultrapatient way adults reserve for recalcitrant children. "Be reasonable."

"No." One little word. So much power. "I don't want your help, Gabriel. I don't need it. I can take care of myself."

"You actually believe that?"

Of course she didn't. Not yet. Not entirely. But she'd beg for change on the street before she'd admit it to him. "Yes. Absolutely."

He stared at her, his expression once again guarded, displaying not a trace of surprise that she'd say something so outrageous. Trapped in the tractor beam of his gaze, with no clue what he was thinking and no words as a distraction, she found herself waiting.

For what, she wasn't sure.

Yet as the silence dragged on, her mind began spinning scenarios. If he wanted to, she mused, he could toss her over his shoulder and simply carry her out of here. Or—the old familiar thrill of awareness slow-danced down her spine—he could walk over, tug her close to that hard, elegant body, tumble her onto the couch and—

"All right, then. I guess we're done."

His flat, uninflected voice startled her out of her

reverie. Yet it still took a good long moment for his actual words to sink in.

That was it? They were done? Really?

For one appalling moment, she didn't know whether to laugh or cry. Then her common sense, which she'd done her best to shun most of her life, kicked in.

Are you crazy? He's throwing in the towel. For heaven's sake, hurry up and hustle him out the door before he changes his mind.

"Well, fancy that," she said with a calculated touch of mockery. "Finally. Something we can agree on."

A nerve jumped in his jaw. "Watch yourself, sweetheart," he advised, even as he took that first wonderful step toward the door. "You know what they say about little girls who poke at predators."

"No. I can't say that I do." She forced herself to stand her ground as he approached, telling herself she was glad this was almost over. He'd go his way, she'd go hers, and in a day, a week, a month, he'd be nothing more than a hazy memory of another life. "Nor, for that matter, do I care—"

With no warning, he crowded close. Startled, she sucked in a breath and tried to scoot out of his way, but it was too late.

He caught her chin in one big hand, tipping her face up to his. "You should," he murmured. "Because the adage goes that eventually the predator strikes back. And eats sweet little things like you—" her stomach flip-flopped at the silky note of warning in his voice "—for lunch."

She swallowed. Hard. Yet somehow her voice sounded almost steady as she fluttered her eyelashes at him and said, "How entertaining. Now let go of me."

"Not yet. There's one other thing we need to get straight."

"Oh? And what is that?"

"When we do have sex—" his gaze flicked to her mouth, lingering before he slowly raised his eyes to hers once again "—it won't have a damn thing to do with payback. Trust me, Mal. You'll be every bit as hot for me as I am for you." And with that he released her as abruptly as he'd caught her and stepped away.

By the time she recovered her breath, he was gone.

Two

Impertinent. Infuriating. Impossible.

   And damn near irresistible.

That pretty much summed up Mallory Morgan, Gabe thought blackly, as he stepped out onto the cracked sidewalk fronting her run-down apartment building. Flipping his coat collar up against the chill March breeze, he checked for traffic on the litter-strewn street, then strode across to his SUV parked on the opposite curb.

He gave the vehicle a cursory look and handed a twenty to the sturdy little Latino kid who'd offered to keep an eye on it for him. "Thanks, *mi'ijo*."

Since their deal had been for ten upfront and ten if

the boy stuck, the youngster's delight was understandable. "*Muchas gracias*, mister!"

Gabe inclined his head. "You earned it."

"*Sí.* So if you come back to Lattimer Street and you need anything, you ask around for Tonio, okay? I take very good care of you."

"I'll keep it in mind."

"*Bueno!*" The kid flashed him a quick grin, then sprinted away as a bus stopped at the far end of the block. Darting around a trio of tattooed street toughs who stood smoking before a boarded-up storefront, he waved as a tired-looking young woman trudged down the steps. "Mama, mama! Guess what?" he exclaimed as he raced toward her through the gathering twilight.

It appeared Gabe had just made somebody's day.

Too freaking bad it was the wrong somebody.

But then, what did he expect? He, who was known for his shrewdness, his finesse, his ability to think outside the box—and yes, dammit, to always be three steps ahead of an opponent—had just behaved with all the subtlety of a Mack truck. He'd invaded Mallory's space, demanded answers, barked orders, bullied when he should've cajoled.

He'd even made a more balls-than-brains promise about their sexual future, for God's sake.

The only thing that kept the day from being a total bust was the very lucrative contract he'd inked at lunch to assess vulnerabilities and tailor protection strategies for the Lux Pacifica hotel chain's overseas executives.

When it came to everything else, however… With

an impatient shake of his head, he put the SUV in gear and set a course for the warehouse district where the Steele Security offices were located. It was slow going due to the Friday night rush hour traffic, affording him plenty of time to think.

There was no excuse for the surprise he'd gotten when he'd walked into Annabelle's and realized the caramel-haired hostess all the men seemed to be admiring was Mallory. Just as there was no rational explanation for how strongly he'd disliked seeing her smoky gaze go from pleasant to hostile at the sight of him.

Given that in the four years he'd known her he'd never seen Mallory get worked up about anything—from being drenched with champagne by a hapless waiter at a Denver symphony opening to strolling onto a balcony at Meg Bender's Halloween party and finding her father getting it on with one of her girlfriends—her ire had gotten his attention. So had her scathing denunciation of him.

But not, as Annabelle's horrified manager had assumed, because he was angry or offended.

No, what had set him back on his heels, what had tested his normally abundant patience as he'd been forced to go ahead with what had seemed like an interminable business luncheon, was the desolation he thought he'd glimpsed under Mallory's anger. That, and the suspicion that her transformation from light-hearted nymphet to go-to-hell working girl meant somewhere along the line he'd made a major miscalculation.

He didn't make miscalculations. Major or otherwise.

That wasn't to say he considered himself infallible. It was just that from his youngest days, after his mother had died and he'd found himself in charge of a brood of eight at the ripe old age of fourteen, mistakes had been a luxury he couldn't afford. That hadn't changed during his years with the military's Special Operations Command.

As for his current circumstances, he hadn't gone from penniless stand-in parent to powerful millionaire businessman due to faulty judgment. No. All that he had, the success, the sterling reputation, the respect of his peers, had come from shrewd vision, meticulous planning, superior instincts and razor-sharp situational awareness.

Not that you'd know by today's performance, he conceded as he finally pulled into Steele Security's underground parking garage.

In his world, where outcome was everything, the fact that Mallory remained ensconced in her squalid little apartment suggested that his decision to chase her down before he'd fully vetted the situation wasn't the smartest move he'd ever made.

Still, honesty forced him to admit that things hadn't gone irredeemably to hell until she'd actually opened her door to him.

To say he'd been caught off guard was an understatement. It had felt more like he'd taken a shot between the eyes with a sledgehammer. Because dear God, the sight of her...

Wrapped in that flimsy siren-red robe, with her feet bare, that streaky brown-and-gold hair mussed and a faint flush tinting her petal-smooth cheeks, she'd looked as if she'd just tumbled out of some lucky man's bed.

Lust had slammed him like a punch to the gut.

By itself, that shouldn't have been a factor since he never allowed his libido to rule his head. But when moments later she'd made a valiant effort to control her trembling lower lip, something inside him had shifted.

What, he couldn't say. But whatever it was, the combination of it and that blast of desire had taken him completely out of his game.

His jaw bunched at the reminder. Climbing out of his vehicle, he punched in the code for the security door and let himself in to the building core, choosing the stairs over the elevator. Once on the main level, he bore left, his long legs eating up the distance as he strode down the wide, airy corridor. He passed by his own spacious office in favor of his brother Cooper's, glad to see the lights were still on.

He ducked his head in the open doorway. "Did you get that information I asked for?"

The younger Steele—number four in the nine-man birth order—glanced over from where he sat slouched in his tilted-back office chair. He was the picture of relaxation with his sneaker-clad feet propped on his desk, an illusion contradicted only by the rapid movement of his fingers over the computer keyboard propped on his lap.

"Do women swoon when I walk into a room?" he responded serenely. "The answer to both questions, big brother, is yes. Of course."

"And?"

"And you're giving me a crick in the neck standing over there. Why don't you come in, take a load off, tell Uncle Cooper what's put the stick up your ass."

Gabe snorted inelegantly. "That'll be the day." Despite his words, he did walk farther into the room, although not to take Cooper up on his invitation. He was here to collect intel, not dispense it. "Well? You going to tell me what you found out or not?"

The younger man shrugged. "Nothing much has changed. The warrant for Cal Morgan's arrest remains active, although my contact at the Feds says it's currently not worth the paper it's printed on. As long as Morgan stays in San Timoteo, they can't touch him, much less a dime of all that stolen money. Which, FYI, my friend now puts at twenty million, meaning that you, once again, win the office pool."

"Terrific." He shrugged out of his coat and tossed it with more force than was necessary onto one of the navy suede chairs in front of the desk. "There's nothing I like better than accurately predicting the extent of a disaster."

"Not your responsibility," Cooper said calmly. "You know damn well it would've been a whole lot worse if we hadn't been brought in when we were."

The hell of it was, Gabe did. And it wasn't that he was the least bit sorry Steele Security had been the one to expose Caleb Morgan's crooked dealings, he admitted, pacing restlessly toward the bank of windows at the far end of the room.

They'd done what they'd been hired to—check out Morgan Creek Investment. And they'd done it the way they did everything, thoroughly and completely.

It hadn't mattered that it wasn't their usual sort of job. Or that their client, a prospective Morgan Creek investor, had only expected them to give the company a quick once-over to placate his elderly mother, who swore that while on a recent trip overseas she'd been unable to locate the Taiwanese shopping mall featured in the company's literature.

The son was now sending his mother flowers weekly, since she'd saved him a bundle when it turned out the mall really didn't exist.

While Morgan, who'd fled the country the day after Steele had clued in the authorities, was most likely sipping mai tais on the veranda of his newly acquired tropical estate, living a life of luxury made possible by the pirated millions he'd socked away in untouchable offshore accounts.

No, if Gabe did have a regret, it was that they hadn't brought the bastard down sooner. While it wouldn't have changed what Morgan had done, it no doubt would have limited the extent of the ensuing damage. As it was, between unpaid taxes and first-position creditors, there hadn't been much left but crumbs for his bilked clients to recover.

And then there was Mallory. Who, until five hours ago, Gabe had assumed was off in St. Croix or Monte

Carlo or some other exotic locale, licking her wounds in luxurious seclusion. Not living all on her own in one of Denver's worst neighborhoods, trying to scrape by on some minimum wage job.

And there it was, that unexpected, unacceptable miscalculation.

"What about Morgan's daughter?" he asked abruptly, swiveling around to stare expectantly at his brother. "What did you find out about her?"

Cooper's busy fingers stilled. "You mean, in addition to the fact that she gave you a shellacking at lunch today?"

"How the hell did you hear about that?"

Cooper rolled his eyes. "How do you think? Family grapevine, bro. Some woman Lilah went to school with saw what happened at Annabelle's and couldn't wait to call Lilah and tell her all about it. Lilah told Dom when he took her to her doctor's appointment, and he told me when he stopped by to pick up the Lederer file on their way home."

"Geezus." The intrabrother communication network had always been good, but the addition in the past year of Gen and Lilah, his sisters-in-law, had definitely kicked it up a notch.

"Yeah. Pretty scary, huh?"

"You could say that. Is Lilah all right? No surprises at the doctor's?" Leaving the windows, he walked back toward Coop's desk.

"As far as I know, she's as good as a woman six months gone can be. Dom, on the other hand, may not make it."

"No news there." Their brother, Dominic, a former

Navy SEAL, had been the embodiment of the brash, tough, never-let-'em-see-you-sweat warrior until he'd signed on to rescue a pretty blond socialite from the banana republic where she was being held prisoner. Now he and Lilah were married and expecting their first child, and he was as overprotective as a five-star general with a troop of one.

"I guess that's true," Cooper conceded. "But still…Lilah mentioned today how much she's enjoying working on some big charity ball, and you could practically see Dom's teeth start to gnash. It seems like the closer she gets to her due date, the harder it is for him to pretend he doesn't want to haul her off somewhere and wrap her in a nice safe protective bubble." He sighed. "If it wasn't so funny, it'd be pathetic. He used to be such a player."

Gabe's dark mood lightened fractionally at his brother's mournful expression. He shrugged. "Love makes people crazy." One of the excellent reasons why it wasn't for him.

"I'll say." Sliding the keyboard onto the desk, he turned his attention back to Gabe, his melancholy vanishing as quickly as it had come. "While we're on the subject of crazy, was the divine Ms. Morgan really working as a waitress?"

"Hostess," Gabe corrected.

"And she actually called you an egotistical, scumsucking sonofabitch?"

"She may have. I wasn't exactly taking notes."

"And?"

"That about covers it. As noted, she called me a few choice names, refused to seat me, then left when her boss tried to smooth over the situation."

"Huh." Cooper eyed him consideringly. "So what did she say when you went after her later? Was she still pissed?"

"Who said I went after her?"

"Please." Cooper sniffed. "You canceled your afternoon appointments, you asked for a Morgan family update, and it's been obvious ever since you walked in here you're tweaked about something. Plus Dom says you two have always had a thing for each other…"

A vision of Mallory's robe drifting south and exposing her smooth, velvet-skinned shoulders flashed through Gabe's mind.

"So yeah," Cooper concluded. "You went after her."

He thrust the vision away. "You're right. I did. And yes, she wasn't exactly thrilled to see me, which given the circumstances is no great surprise. As for the rest of what we discussed…"

He thought about Mallory's attempt to act indifferent about her situation while foolishly insisting she was doing just fine, and once more felt frustrated, impatient, annoyed—and yes, although he couldn't quite figure out why—touched.

"It's none of your business."

"Aw, come on. Don't tell me you're going to stonewall your favorite sibling."

"Hell, no. But then, last I checked, Deke's still in Borneo."

"Ouch." Cooper gave him a faux-wounded look. "You could've just said no."

"Like you've ever let that word stop you? Give me a break." Leaning over, he planted his hands on his brother's desk. "And as much as I'd love to share my innermost feelings, hear all about your and Dom's riveting take on my love life—" with each word his voice acquired a little more bite "—it's after six and I have plans for tonight. So what do you say you just tell me what I want to know, and we leave the rest for another time? Say, the next time you girls have a slumber party?"

Cooper made a reproachful face. "No need to get surly."

Silent, Gabe continued to stare down at him.

"Okay, okay," he said hastily, raising his hands in mock surrender. "Here goes. Up until six months ago, our subject was holed up at the family estate, even though the staff had been let go months before that. Then, when the Feds finally came in, seized everything and locked the place down, she checked into the Markham Plaza. She was there for several weeks, until her credit card was declined and they found out it was no mistake. Word is she tried to make good with a check, but it bounced, too, and the management not so kindly asked her to leave."

Straightening, he consulted his computer monitor. "Her credit report shows two different apartment management firms checked her history the following week. Considering that she had an extensive collection of plastic, but that every single card was closed due to late or no payments, several with substantial balances, I'm guessing they passed on renting to her."

Considering where she'd wound up living, Gabe imagined he was right.

"The interesting thing is, except for a small portion of one account, everything else was paid off a few weeks later. And she was making the bare-bones payment on that last outstanding debt until roughly sixty days ago, when she also started to fall behind on her rent."

Gabe frowned, trying to make sense of it. "What about bank accounts?" he asked, pushing upright and starting to pace.

"Checking account was closed due to overdrafts. Nothing else popped, but then I didn't have enough time to do much more than skim the surface. Does it matter?"

"Probably not. It's just that I thought—" incorrectly, it appeared, although it was still the main reason he hadn't seen fit to check up on her before "—she had a trust fund, a substantial one. She says it's long gone."

Cooper frowned. "You don't believe her?"

"I didn't say that. But I want to be sure." Despite the overwhelming evidence that Mallory was operating without a safety net, this time around he wasn't assuming anything.

"I'll have another look."

"Thanks."

"Anything else?"

"No. I'd say that does it for now."

Cooper drummed his fingers on the desk. "I take it that means you're not done with Mallory? Even though, from the sound of things, she ranks you somewhere below foot fungus on the list of things she could live without?"

"What's your point, Coop? Assuming you have one?"

"I do." Never shy about stating his opinion, he met Gabe's narrow stare straight on. "Look, I know how committed you are, not just to making this business a success, but to doing your best to ensure that the work we all do matters. That whenever possible, we do what we can to make peoples' lives safer and better.

"Because of that, I think you need a reminder that no matter what this woman said to you, no matter how hard she may have tried to guilt trip you, she's not your responsibility—and you definitely don't owe her anything."

"Believe me." Gabe smiled sardonically. "That's not the problem here."

Cooper looked surprised. "No? Then what—"

"Leave it alone, little brother. I appreciate your concern, but I've been successfully conducting my own affairs for a whole lot of years now. If I decide I need help, from you or the rest of the family, I'll be sure to let you know. In the meantime—" shooting his cuff, he glanced at his wristwatch "—the clock is ticking and I'm sure I've got a stack of things to take care of before I can get out of here."

"That's it? You're just going to walk?"

"Pretty much." Reaching down, he snagged his coat off the chair and deliberately steered the conversation in a different direction. "You going out to Taggart and Gen's for dinner tomorrow?"

To his credit, Cooper knew when to throw in the towel. "Are you kidding? Free, home-cooked meal along with Rockies Cactus League ball on the tube?" He sat back and again propped his feet up. "I'm there. What about you?"

"Yeah, I'm in, too." He headed toward the door. "You want to share a ride?"

"Sure."

"I'll call you tomorrow, we can hash out the details." Reaching the doorway, he paused. "Hey, Coop?"

"What?"

"Thanks for the information. I appreciate it."

"Easy for you to say," the younger man groused, but without any heat. "You're not the one left hanging."

"I think you'll survive," he said drily. And with that, he headed down the hall toward his own office and what was sure to be a fat folder of items needing his attention, reassured by the knowledge that Cooper's bad temper wouldn't last past the next five minutes.

Knowing as well that while his brother's concern for him had been misplaced, the younger Steele had been right about one thing.

Gabe wasn't done with Mallory. Not by a long shot.

Three

"Are you all right, Miss Morgan?"

Mallory dragged her gaze from the rectangle of paper clutched in her trembling hand to stare blankly at the man seated across from her. "What?"

Mr. Cowden's thin, intelligent face softened. "You seem a bit shaken," the owner of Finders Keepers, the search firm she'd been contacted by the previous day, observed not unkindly. "Can I get you something? A glass of water? Some coffee?"

"No. I... It's just..." Embarrassed to find herself babbling, she pressed her lips together and struggled for composure. "Please, could you explain to me again where this came from? You said it's a behest from a relative?"

"Yes. According to the letter we received, the funds originated with—" he glanced down at the paper centered atop his glossy walnut desk "—one Ivan Mallory Milton. Your cousin, it seems, although most likely a distant one since it states here he was ninety-one at the time he expired. The family connection—" he adjusted his glasses and scanned further down the document "—was apparently through your maternal grandmother."

"But I've never even heard of him."

"Well, yes, that's actually rather common with this sort of distant connection. And truthfully, as you might imagine, quite often inheritances go unclaimed for just that reason. In this case," he said, tapping a finger against the paper, "it seems that Mr. Milton first realized the relationship after reading a newspaper article about your family."

Mallory winced. Given her father's notoriety and the extensive press coverage he'd received, she didn't imagine that anything her late cousin had read would have been complimentary. Not that that appeared to have made a difference.

"The information was found among his belongings after he passed away, and since he had no other heirs, it was determined these funds should come to you. Although these days, with the popularity of the Internet, it is rather unusual for us to be contacted through the regular mail this way…."

Even as she told herself she should pay attention to what Mr. Cowden was saying, Mallory's gaze drifted back to the cashier's check.

Sure enough, right after Pay To The Order Of was her name, followed by the fabulous, wonderful, miraculous sum of four thousand, seven hundred, twenty-one dollars and forty-six cents.

A year ago, that amount wouldn't have qualified as her monthly shoe allowance. Now it meant she could take a deep breath for the first time in months. And she owed it all to someone she'd never met, and never would.

Thank you, dear departed cousin Ivan.

Not, she thought hastily, that she was glad her long-lost relative was dead. But if the old guy had to go, she certainly couldn't fault his timing.

"Miss Morgan?"

With a start, she realized her companion was staring at her quizzically, as though he'd stopped speaking some time ago and was waiting for a response. "I'm sorry," she said hastily. "It's just this—" she smoothed her thumb over the crease in the paper caused by the overly enthusiastic grip of her fingers "—I can't quite take it in. It's such a surprise."

"But a welcome one, surely." Smiling, Mr. Cowden came to his feet.

"Oh, yes." It was so welcome she couldn't quite believe somebody wasn't going to pop out of the woodwork at any second, claim there'd been a mistake and snatch her windfall away.

"I can't tell you how much that pleases me," he went on as he came around the desk. "And how glad I am that we were able to be of assistance. Frankly," his blue eyes gleamed cheerfully, "this is always my favorite part of the job."

"I can understand why." With a smile of her own, she carefully folded the check and slid it into the inner compartment of her purse for safekeeping. Since it was obvious from Mr. Cowden's behavior that he considered their business done, she stood, as well. "Do I owe you something? Isn't there a fee for you finding me?"

"Yes, of course there is, but it's already been taken care of by Mr. Milton's representative." He held her coat for her, then ushered her through the door into the outer office. Minutes later, after signing a paper acknowledging receipt of the money, and a round of thank-yous, good lucks and goodbyes, she found herself standing outside on the sidewalk in the midmorning sunshine.

For one glorious moment, elation got the better of her and she actually did a twirl. Four thousand, seven hundred and twenty-one dollars! She couldn't seem to wipe the smile off her face as she waltzed up the street toward the bus stop, her feet barely touching the ground, her mind filled with possibilities.

Where, oh where, to start? Tres Chic for a facial, a massage, a full day of beauty? Heaven knew, her pores would thank her. Or Mr. Kenneth's to pamper her hair with some highlights and one of his signature haircuts? Should she make a trip to Marchant's and pick up that to-die-for Moreno handbag she'd seen in the window last week? Or spring for a new pair of Merrazi wedges since a toddler with attitude had stomped on the toe of her favorites her first day at Annabelle's?

Maybe the order of the day was to go out for a lei-surely lunch. Or, even better, treat herself to an elegant dinner. It would feel good to get all dressed up. Although most of her clothes had gone for consign-ment, she still had a few nice things. She could catch a cab to Gambiolini's and request her usual table, then while away a few hours sipping a glass or two of pricey red wine, flirting with Phillippe, her favorite waiter, in-dulging her months-long craving for the house spe-cialty, shrimp tettrazini.

Except somebody she knew was bound to be there. Did she really want to deal with the whispers and re-pressive stares or, even worse, the humiliation of being treated as if she were invisible?

Okay, so maybe dinner out wasn't the best idea, she decided, as her bus pulled up. No matter. There were all sorts of other ways she could amuse herself. Like getting her good wristwatch back from the pawnshop, she thought as her bus pulled up and she instinctively checked the time on its drugstore replacement.

Climbing on board, she flashed her pass at the driver, walked back to her accustomed seat in the middle, and continued to dream.

She could rent a car and make the trip to Aurora to make sure her favorite jumper was doing all right with his new owner. Top Flight had always been a challenge, part of the reason she'd loved him, and it would be good to know that he'd settled into his new surround-ings.

For that matter, she could drive up to Breckenridge

and spend a few days skiing and being pampered at The Pinnacle, one of her favorite little ultraluxury spa resorts. Although she supposed she should probably call first. It wasn't unusual for them to be booked an entire season in advance.

Of course, before she went anywhere or called anyone, she needed to pay her overdue cell bill—something else she could now afford to do. Just think! For the first time in what felt like forever, she wasn't going to have to worry that her phone service, an absolute essential to job hunting, not to mention her sense of safety, was about to be cut off.

Heck, once her account was cleared she'd even be able to use some of her precious minutes on nonessential calls, such as letting Gabriel know—again—that she didn't want or need his help. Even better—the thought of it had her sitting up straighter—she could send him the money to pay for the locksmith who'd shown up the day after their encounter to install locks on her doors and windows.

She still wasn't sure what she resented most about the gesture. The hit to her pride that with a snap of his elegant fingers he could dispatch someone to take care of something she herself had been unable to afford? Or that she could no longer crawl into bed without thinking about him because, for the first time since moving into the place, she was actually getting some sleep instead of constantly jolting awake at each and every little noise? Even though the night after the locks had gone on she'd bolted awake to hear someone fruitlessly trying to force her front door?

Or was the agitation she felt when she thought of him caused by something else entirely? Perhaps a secret fear that hiring the locksmith had been his parting gesture? Could it be that deep down she was really afraid he'd taken her at her word and intended to respect her request that he stay away?

Absolutely not, she thought, squaring her shoulders. Sure, she was surprised he hadn't been back to harass her. But why shouldn't she be? He didn't seem like the sort of man to back down from anything. And his parting shot *had* seemed to indicate that as far as he was concerned, they were far from finished.

Which was just plain crazy, given that they'd never started. Certainly they'd been friends of a sort, and she couldn't deny that they'd always had chemistry, but they'd both chosen never to cross the line into something more. And while she'd obviously had her reasons for keeping him at arm's length—he *so* wasn't the type for a superficial dalliance—he'd quite clearly kept his distance for reasons of his own.

Reasons she'd never really thought about.

And wasn't about to start now, she told herself firmly. For too many years she'd been like a leaf in the stream going wherever the current took her, coasting over bumps, sliding around obstacles, letting outside elements determine her path.

Well, she was done with that. Like it or not, it was up to her whether she wound up over her head in some stagnant pool or learned how to keep herself afloat.

That was why, she realized, coming back to earth as

she stared out the window at a cityscape that was getting drearier with every passing block, she wasn't going to spend cousin Ivan's money on anything foolish like designer shoes or salon haircuts or pricey vacations. For the very first time since she'd found herself stranded outside the Plaza with no one to call and nowhere to go, she had a cushion, however small, between herself and life on the street.

She wasn't about to blow it. No, except to take care of her overdue rent and phone bill and purchase some urgently needed groceries, the new, improved Mallory was going to sock that money away and continue to watch every last nickel, dime and penny.

She was certain she wouldn't have to do it indefinitely. After all, a mystery relative unexpectedly bequeathing her money had to be a sign that her luck was changing. So tomorrow she would again scour the papers for jobs, hit the streets, renew her quest to join the ranks of the gainfully employed.

And surely, if she just tried hard enough, by this time next week she was bound to be somebody's favorite new employee.

Stripper. Nursing home attendant. Fast-food worker.

That pretty much described her current career path, Mallory thought dejectedly as she climbed off the bus well after dark a week later.

Pulling her coat a little tighter against the chill from the snow that had begun falling in the past hour, she began to pick her way home through the freezing slush in her too-thin pumps, sincerely wishing that she'd had the foresight to wear boots when she'd left that morning.

Of course, at the time, the weather had been warm and sunny, matching her mood as she set out to apply for half a dozen promising employment possibilities.

Now, twelve long hours later, after riding eight different buses, walking dozens of blocks, and an eternity of waiting, talking, smiling and praying, not one job offer had come her way.

But then, the positions she'd applied for had actually paid a livable salary, instead of minimum wage for part-time hours too sparse to cover the barest necessities like rent or food. As an added bonus, they also hadn't required her to breathe heavily into a phone or take her clothes off in front of strangers.

And so far, with the exception of the hostess gig at Annabelle's, which she'd so foolishly thrown away, those seemed to be the only kind of offers she could generate.

Not that she was feeling sorry for herself or anything, she thought, jumping a little as a door slammed in the distance and an unseen man screamed an obscenity. Okay, so maybe her inability to find decent employment was making her feel even more useless than normal. And she couldn't seem to stop thinking about how close to living under a bridge she'd be if not for last week's windfall.

And yes, her feet were freezing, the too-quiet, seemingly deserted street was creeping her out and the thought of spending another night eating boxed mac and cheese all alone in her drafty apartment made her feel beyond bleak, but—

"Well, look what the cat dragged in."

Her head snapped up as a tall, menacing figure materialized out of an unlit doorway in front of her. She slid to a stop, her heart jamming into her throat as the interloper stepped squarely into her path.

Time slowed, then ceased, while her thoughts splintered. *Run!* screamed through her along with *ohmigod I'm going to die* at the same time an oddly detached little voice murmured, *Gee, doesn't that voice sound sort of familiar?*

Then the man took a threatening step closer and the snow-dappled light from the streetlamp on the corner touched his face and her heart lurched back to life.

"Have you lost your *mind*?" Dragging desperately needed air into her constricted lungs, she didn't think, just reacted, lunging forward to smack Gabriel in his big, broad, not-even-breathing-hard chest. "Of all the mean, rotten, low-down dirty tricks! You scared me half to death—"

"*Good.*" His warm fingers braceleted her flailing wrists. "You should be scared, dammit!" Even in the dark, there was no mistaking his grim expression. "What the hell are you doing out here at this hour?"

"Gosh, let me think. Oh, I know—I live here!"

"Well, here's a news flash," he shot back, effortlessly reeling her closer as she tried to pull free. "You won't be living anywhere if you don't have better sense than to tiptoe around after dark with your head bowed like some scared little mouse. God, Mallory! Don't you have enough sense to know that in a neighborhood like this, any display of weakness is an invitation to be mugged—or worse?"

"You mean like having to fend off some know-it-all wannabe stalker?"

He leaned into her, so close she could feel the warm wash of his breath on her icy skin. "Believe me, sweetheart. If I were stalking you, there wouldn't be any wannabe about it."

Maybe it was the delicious tickle of terror evoked by his words. Or the sight of that hard, chiseled mouth mere inches from her own. But in a flash, awareness roared to life, crowding out her anger. She registered his heat, his size, the strength of the hands dwarfing her own.

Her throat went tight. And try as she might to tell herself it was a delayed reaction to the fright she'd received, no way did that explain the overwhelming urge she had to crowd closer and give herself over to his potent masculine power—

"Dammit, you're shivering." Abruptly, he released her. Relief streaked through her, only to be snuffed out as he whipped off his coat and wrapped it around her. "Come on." His voice was as hard as the arm suddenly looping her waist, urging her forward. "Let's get you in out of this cold."

She thought of her apartment, and the idea of being trapped in that small, intimate space with him had her digging in her heels. "I'm fine. Really. And you can drop the concerned act because I'm absolutely not inviting you in—"

"No problem. My car's right here."

"What?" She tried to struggle as he unlocked the door of a big black SUV, only to find that his enveloping coat was as confining as a straitjacket. "No, Gabriel. While I understand your compelling need to put your hands on me—" she gamely tried to infuse some of the old flippancy into her voice "—it's been a really long day."

"We need to talk." He opened the door and planted his free hand on the roof of the car, neatly boxing her in. "So either we go inside to your place where it'll be just the two of us or you get in the car and we drive to some nice, public restaurant. You decide."

It was no choice at all, and he knew it. Yet it was also clear he wasn't going away. "Fine. We'll go to the restaurant." Giving him a narrow-eyed stare, she allowed him to help her up onto the seat. "But this had better be brief."

He said nothing to that, simply shut the door, walked around and got in on the other side.

Five miles and what felt like another world later, they were seated across from each other at a booth in a cozy little diner that came complete with checked curtains on the windows, a bell over the door and an array of mouthwatering scents wafting from the kitchen.

"Hungry?" he asked as the waitress arrived with her pad.

Mallory shrugged, ignoring the sudden grinding of her empty stomach. "Not really." Dinner out simply didn't figure into her budget. Not when she had food at home, and the twenty dollars in her wallet was supposed to last her through the end of the week.

He studied her a moment, then turned to the waitress. "Two coffees, the chicken fried steak for me and a chef salad for the lady." Switching his attention back to Mallory, he ignored her look of disbelief. "I'm buying," he informed her matter-of-factly. "Now, what kind of dressing do you want?" When she simply continued to stare at him, he gave a slight shrug. "Make it Thousand Island," he told the bemused server.

"Make it blue cheese," she contradicted. If she was going to eat, she might as well get what she liked. "And I'd rather have tea instead of coffee, please. And separate checks, if you would." She'd just have to skip lunch during her job hunt the next few days.

The waitress, a stout, pleasant-faced woman in her forties, wisely refrained from comment. She asked a few order-related questions, brought their drinks, then hustled off to post their order and take care of the rest of her tables.

Mallory gave the tea time to steep, then wrapped her hands around the cup and took a sip, hoping to counteract the exhaustion that was suddenly sweeping through her.

Gabe looked over at her, far too astute for comfort. "You all right?"

She sat up a little straighter. "You mean, except for having been so rudely snatched off the street?"

"Yes. Except for that."

"I'm fine."

"You mentioned that it had been a long day. Where were you, anyway?"

She might be tired but she wasn't dead, and she certainly wasn't discussing her failure on the employment front. She fluttered her eyelashes. "Where else? I was off meeting Raoul, my secret lover."

"Ah." He took a sip of his coffee. "He must be a real prize to send you home on the bus."

She shrugged. "What can I say? He's French."

"My sincere condolences." His tone was perfectly solemn, but those jewel-tone eyes suddenly gleamed with a touch of laughter.

It was unexpected. And shockingly attractive. Just like him, she thought, studying that symmetrical, good-looking face. The strong cheekbones, level eyebrows and sensual mouth were enough to turn any woman's head. But it was the self-assurance, the surety of purpose, the wicked intelligence that held her gaze.

She felt the pull of his appeal clear to her toes. It didn't mean anything, of course. She was simply experiencing the ever-present hum of awareness she felt whenever she was near him.

And if perhaps there was something more? If, as their gazes meshed in that moment of shared humor, she inexplicably felt connected to him?

An illusion, she told herself sharply. One she couldn't afford to indulge. Lifting her cup to her mouth, she used the movement as an excuse to look away. "Why were you waiting for me tonight, anyway?"

There was a moment's silence. "I came to give you

this." Pulling out his wallet, he extracted two hundred-dollar bills and three twenties—the exact amount of the money order she'd sent him to pay for the locksmith—and held it out.

"Then you wasted a trip," she said, making no move to take it. "I'm grateful for the thought, but as it happens I recently received an unexpected windfall so I can afford to pay for—"

"No." For a second his mouth tightened with exasperation, then his expression smoothed out. "I'm not taking your money, Mallory. Not for a meal I coerced you into ordering. And certainly not for hardware and labor—" before she could stop him, he picked up her purse, opened it and tucked the cash into an inside pocket "—for a job you didn't have any control over."

"That's not true," she said instantly, telling herself she'd just leave the money in his car later if he refused to see reason now. "I could've refused to let your man in."

"Yes, you could. But it wouldn't have made any difference. As I believe Sonny told you, he had his orders."

"He said if I didn't let him install the locks, you'd make sure he got fired."

"Ah." Gabe steepled his fingers. "Well, there you have it."

There was something in his voice, and she eyed him suspiciously. "It wasn't true?"

"Let's just say it would be tough to do since Sonny owns the business."

"Ohmigod," she breathed. "You two played me. Doesn't it bother you that I think you're that ruthless?"

"Not if it makes you safer."

The easy statement stole her breath. At the very least she ought to be angered by his high-handedness, disgusted by the deception, indignant at his interference. Instead, she was stunned by the idea that he actually seemed to care what happened to her. God knows, her own father hadn't.

That's right. The thought put a little starch back in her spine. *So instead of getting all fluttery inside and doing a Sally Field, this would be an excellent time to remember that no matter what Gabriel does, you still have to learn how to take care of yourself.*

Misreading her silence, he raised a hand. "Just so there's no misunderstanding, since you always seem to think I've got an ulterior motive, I'm not saying that just to get into your pants." His eyes glinted, but this time it wasn't humor lighting them up. "Not tonight anyway."

She tried to ignore the flicker of heat generated by his threat—or was it a promise?—that there'd be another time, and focus on all the questions that still remained between them. Yet before she could do either one, the waitress arrived with their food.

It smelled fabulous, and with a slight jolt, she realized three things simultaneously.

Call her a wimp, but she'd had all the responsibility she could handle for one day. Being a grown-up was hard work, and between having to weigh every dime she spent, looking for a job and questioning every word that came out of Gabriel's mouth, she was just plain worn-out with it. Surely, the world wouldn't come to an end if she took a time-out and simply enjoyed herself for a measly half hour.

She supposed it also wouldn't tilt off its axis if she allowed Gabe one small victory and let him pay for her meal.

The last was that she was a lot hungrier than she'd thought.

So it seemed only fitting, after the waitress served her salad, to slide the mound of lettuce across the table, then reach up and intercept Gabe's plate. "I'll take that, thanks."

The woman didn't so much as blink. "You bet, honey," she said, making a hasty retreat.

Not missing a beat, Mallory slid her fork into the creamy mound of mashed potatoes, slipped it into her mouth and practically moaned with appreciation. "This is wonderful." She took another blissful bite before finally venturing a glance to see how Gabriel was taking the theft of his food.

To her surprise, he was watching her with the strangest look on his face.

One that vanished with the droll twitch of his lips. "Glad you're enjoying it," he said drily as he reached for the salad dressing.

It was the last thing either of them said for quite a while.

Four

"Wow." With a murmured sigh of pleasure, Mallory stretched her feet toward the stream of warm air blasting from the SUV's heater. "That second piece of pie may have been a mistake. I feel like a boa constrictor that swallowed a goat."

Gabe took his eyes off the road to glance over at her. Her heavily lashed eyes were closed, her shining hair tumbled, while her fine-boned profile was a perfect silhouette against the snow-lit night beyond the windows.

She didn't look a thing like the minx who'd hijacked his dinner, then devoured it with such hedonistic pleasure that at one point she'd even licked her spoon.

Instead, she was a dead ringer for a patrician young queen who'd taken a night off from some palace intrigue. Or—his gaze flicked to her mouth—an ultra-exclusive, high-priced courtesan taking a break from the scores of men vying for her attention.

The lust that had dogged him all night pounced, jaws snapping closed like a vise.

He wanted to touch her, dammit. He wanted to skim his palm over her silken jaw, rub the pad of his thumb against those soft, full lips, bury his face in the curling mass of that burnished hair.

Bury himself in her hot silky sex.

Except any one of those moves might accurately be construed as an attempt to get into her pants. Which he, in his infinite wisdom, had promised wasn't on this evening's agenda.

He yanked his gaze back to the street, his mouth twisting at the irony. He'd had, after all, abundant op-portunity in the past to make a move on her. Yet he'd always chosen to pass, for reasons as varied as they were numerous.

He'd been too busy working. She'd been too busy playing.

He'd had younger brothers to raise, a business to run, a host of responsibilities. She'd had none.

He'd preferred his sexual liaisons to be straightfor-ward, a pleasurable exchange between two responsible adults with no strings and no messy complications.

There'd never been anything uncomplicated about Mallory. Then or now.

"Gabriel?" Her voice cut through his thoughts. As if on cue, in a quicksilver shift of mood she suddenly sounded serious, the levity of the previous moment gone.

"What?"

"Why did you come so see me tonight? Really?"

"I told you. The check—"

"No." Cutting him off, she tucked a knee underneath her and shifted on the seat to face him. "If that was your only purpose you could have dropped the thing in the mail or called to tell me you'd destroyed it. You didn't have to show up in person."

"Okay." He inclined his head. "You got me. I wanted to make sure you were okay. I told you before that you don't belong in this neighborhood, and earlier tonight, on the street, you proved my point."

She ignored the provocation of that last statement. "All right. But why do you care? Why now, when I've been living here for months?"

"It's no great mystery, Mallory. Until we ran into each other last week, I didn't know you needed help. Now I do."

"And you feel compelled to provide it?"

"That's not exactly how I'd put it, but yes."

He heard her breathe in, then carefully exhale. "Is it because of my father? Do you feel guilty for exposing him?"

For a second he was tempted to dance around the question. After all, as Gabe had personal reason to know, kids made all sorts of excuses for parents, defending behavior that was often indefensible.

But on this issue, at least, he felt he owed her the truth. "Hell, no," he said flatly. "You may not want to hear this, but it's my firm opinion that your father ought to be in prison. Not off living the high life, working on his tan at a lot of other people's expense."

"Oh."

Braced as he was for a much more vocal protest, her one-word response caught him off guard. Still, he figured they might as well get past this hurdle now.

Pulling up to the curb in front of her building, he switched off the engine and turned to face her, "Oh what, Mallory? Oh, I really am the cold-blooded bastard you thought I was?"

That lush courtesan's mouth unexpectedly curved up for an instant. "How about, oh, I still don't get it? Because if you're not here because of my father and you don't want sex, then what's the draw, Gabriel? Why do you care what happens to me?"

"Why shouldn't I?" He made a note to kick himself later for the whole sex debacle. "We're friends, or at least, we were—"

"No." She shook her head. "We weren't. Maybe it's not exactly my area of expertise—" her voice took on that familiar note of self-mockery "—but even I know that friends spend time together, and talk, and know about each other's dreams and quirks and even some of their secrets. You and I… We were more social acquaintances with a long-standing jones for each other."

He should've been gratified by her acknowledgment of the attraction between them. So why, instead, did her dispassionate dismissal of a broader connection grate like a handful of sand scrubbed across glass? "There's more to it than that. But my point is, while your father deserves the worst the system can throw at him, you…you were just an innocent bystander in all this. Yet somehow you wound up taking the hit for him, and no matter how you view it—a miscarriage of justice, a monumental screwup—it never should've happened."

"So that makes me…what? Collateral damage?"

If he hadn't been so caught up in choosing his next words, her utter lack of inflection might have warned him he'd made a major misstep. "Sure, I suppose you could say that. The label isn't important. What matters is that it's not acceptable. You shouldn't have to lose everything while he skates."

"And you're here to fix that?"

"Yes." Flashing on her reaction every other time he'd tried to offer his assistance, he thought it wise to add, "If you'll let me."

"I see." She slid her feet back into her discarded pumps, her face hidden by the gently curling mass of her hair as she leaned forward. "Well, here's your answer." Straightening, she swiveled to face him, her eyes dark with something he couldn't identify—and anger so blatant a blind man couldn't have missed it. "Go to hell."

She snatched up her purse, shoved open the door and had her feet planted squarely on the pavement outside almost before he could decide what to do.

Almost, but not quite. "I don't think so." He was out

his door and around the vehicle so fast she didn't manage to get more than a few feet before he caught up with her.

"What the hell is your problem!" he demanded, catching her by the elbow and swinging her around.

"You!" she shot back. "You arrogant, self-satisfied jerk!" Sucking in a breath, she yanked her arm free. "In what universe do you think I'd *ever* agree to be your pet project?"

"What?"

"Either you're hard of hearing, or just so full of yourself that nothing can penetrate that incredibly thick hide, so let me spell it out. I don't want your pity or your charity. And I am not, nor will I ever be, some wrong you need to right!"

"Is that what you think?" He couldn't remember the last time he'd completely lost his temper, but he could feel it beginning to go. And it seriously pissed him off. He ruled his emotions. They didn't rule him.

"Yes!" She started to whirl away, then thought better of it. "And just so there's no mistake—" she jerked her handbag open, fumbled around for something inside "—I don't need your damned money, either!" Crumpling the bills that had appeared in her hand, she hurled them at him.

He didn't think, he acted. Trained to always take control of an attack, he snatched the money out of the air, wrapped an arm around her waist and yanked her close.

Mistake. The warning went off in his mind like a Klaxon the instant he felt her plastered against him, all slim curves and yielding flesh. He drew in a breath, but that was a mistake, too, as her scent filled his head, a faint trace of exotic flowers and something that was exclusively, erotically Mallory.

Like a bomb going off, temper exploded into something much, much hotter.

He tossed the money to the ground. Fisting his hand in the heavy silk of her hair, he tipped back her head and claimed her mouth.

If she resisted, it was for the barest second. Then with a shaky little sound that made every muscle in his body tighten, she crowded closer, wound her arms around his neck and hungrily kissed him back.

God, those lips. Sleek, plump, soft, so soft. How often over the years had he wondered how she'd taste, how she'd feel?

Now he knew. And he, who prided himself on always being in control, wasn't.

He wanted to plunder, possess, eat her up.

And touch. Limited by their layers of clothing, he settled for sliding his hand out of her hair to cup the curve of her jaw, trail the pad of his thumb down to the shallow notch at the base of her throat. Her skin felt like satin, and his breathing sped up as he imagined her naked. He knew with a certainty he didn't question she'd be silk soft all over.

He raked his teeth against her bottom lip. She shuddered, then the damp tip of her tongue strafed his upper lip and every Y chromosome in his body stood up and howled.

Bending his knees, he slid his arm from her waist to the firm undercurve of her ass, boosting her up to give himself better access. With another needy little sound she clamped her thighs against his hips.

It was all the encouragement he needed to slide his tongue into the hot sweetness of her mouth. She widened her lips, inviting him deeper, meeting each thrust of his with a welcoming one of her own until he felt as if the top of his head was going to blow off. And still the kiss grew hotter, more demanding, an act of possession that had some primitive part of his brain calculating the number of feet to the SUV's wide backseat.

Yet even as he pictured himself laying her down, stripping away her clothes, the protector in him registered the sound of a door opening somewhere up the street. It was followed by a chorus of adolescent male voices raised in a mixture of taunts and laughter that was slowly drifting closer.

As a former military officer, he knew all about young men, rampaging hormones, the pack mentality. Add in that these youngsters were more likely to be gangbangers than Boy Scouts and he had to wonder—

What the *hell* was he doing? Since when did he forget his surroundings to make out on a darkened sidewalk in a bad part of town?

A week ago the answer would've been never. But not anymore.

Not since Mallory had somehow managed to turn him inside out and upside down.

That was no excuse for him behaving like a

hormonal teenager himself, however. Much less acting in a way that could draw unwanted attention her way, jeopardizing her safety.

He brought his head up, breaking their contact, and abruptly set her on her feet. "Mal." His voice was harsh with the cost of his reacquired restraint.

"Hmm?" She stared blankly at him.

He steadied her as she swayed. "Come home with me."

"What?" Although her voice was still a velvety rasp, her passion-dazed eyes were starting to clear.

"It's late, it's cold, you shouldn't be here by yourself." He ignored the little voice that urged him to just shut up, throw her over his shoulder and cart her back to his cave. "Come home with me," he repeated. "We can sort things out in the morning."

"I—" She took a jerky step back. "No. I—" She dampened her lips with her tongue and to his chagrin it was all he could do not to groan out loud. "*Ohmigod. I can't believe I just did that. That I let you…*" She made a strangled sound and retreated another step, nearly tripping over her forgotten handbag, which at some point she'd dropped on the ground.

He reached out to catch her and she wrenched away. "Don't," she said sharply, scooping the purse from the snowy slush and clutching it to her breasts like a shield. "I…I need to go."

The hell of it was, unless she was going to miraculously change her mind and get in the car, she was right.

Not that she appeared to require his permission. Turning on her heel, she fled toward her building, wrenched open the main door with its useless lock and disappeared out of sight inside, leaving him alone in the night.

He waited until the lights in her unit went on, standing his ground as the small group of teenagers finally sauntered by, jostling and talking trash to each other, yet giving him a wide berth. Intuitively they seemed to know it would be an extremely bad idea to tangle with him.

Not until the boys rounded the corner and the street was quiet once again did he turn and start for his car. He was almost to the curb when something on the ground caught his eye.

Bending down, he saw it was the money Mallory had tossed at him. He picked it up and straightened. Smoothing the bills out, he saw that in her anger she'd only managed to hurl about half of the cash he'd returned to her back at him.

He supposed he ought to be glad she hadn't tossed the whole damn purse at him.

The errant thought brought a faint smile to his mouth. It grew nominally wider as he considered the implication of the dazed look that had been on her face when he'd had to set her away from him. No matter what she might say in the future, she wanted him.

And he wanted her. Not for forever, he thought as he folded the cash and slipped it into his breast pocket. Forever was a very long time, and at this stage in his life, after devoting most of the past twenty years to his brothers' welfare, he didn't see himself signing on for more than right now with anyone.

But that didn't mean he was just going to walk away from what he wanted, either.

Five

"Now let me see…" An insincere smile on her flaw-lessly made-up face, Nikki Victor-Volpe looked away from Mallory to contemplate her immaculately mani-cured fingertips. "You worked on Bedazzled in some capacity for how long…?"

"Nine years," Mallory replied steadily, even though she knew perfectly well that Nikki already knew the answer. Both of them had volunteered to work on the event during their junior year at the exclusive private prep school they'd both attended, where a public service stint was a graduation requirement.

But even if Nikki had suffered a temporary brain lapse—not, Mallory supposed, completely out of the realm of possibility considering the amount of empty space in the blonde's expensively coiffed head—the information was also in the extensive application she'd had Mallory fill out.

The one visible in the opened folder on Nikki's lap.

Mallory reminded herself that being made to jump through Nikki's little hoops didn't matter, not compared to how much she wanted this job. The Bedazzled Ball was the most prestigious of Denver's charity events, a mammoth black-tie affair that raised a huge amount of money each year for a worthy local cause.

While most of the work was done by volunteers, the job of event coordinator was a paid position. And though the coordinator put in mostly part-time hours up until the months directly preceding the event, the job came with a prorated salary since it was normally filled after the previous year's ball.

Now, with only six weeks to go until the big night, the position had suddenly become available. While that was unusual in itself, the fact that someone on the steering committee had thought of Mallory as a potential replacement and had instructed Nikki, the committee secretary, to call and ask if she'd be interested, was a miracle.

One she intended to try her best to capitalize on. That's why she'd spent hours at the library yesterday reading everything she could about the charity. It was the reason she'd changed clothes six times this morning before settling on exactly the right outfit and shown up at Bedazzled's downtown offices for her interview forty minutes early.

Because not only did she really, really want this job, she *needed* it. For the obvious reason—she was desperate for gainful employment—but also because it would give her some much-needed experience to add to her résumé, a chance to do work that was actually meaningful, and a shot, however slim, at landing a similar, hopefully longer-term position in the future.

It was just an added bonus that it might also help her forget the blinding speed with which she'd turned into a sex-crazed nymphomaniac at the first touch of Gabriel's lips.

His hot, hard, drugging, lay-me-down-and-do-me lips.

Oh, God. Heat twisted through her despite the chilly temperature of the conference room where she and Nikki sat. Without even closing her eyes she could recall the weight of his hand in her hair, the warm roughness of his palm sliding over her throat, the heady taste of his tongue moving against her own. And the singular sensation of the dense, steely muscles in his chest and abdomen flexing against her front as he'd lifted her up, pressing her against his—

No, no, no. She absolutely wasn't going there. Not here, not now, not again. It was bad enough that she seemed to be incapable of purging her mind of those thigh-clenching memories. But what did it say about her character that the episode could intrude into her thoughts at such a crucial time?

Maybe that you were right all those years to fear your attraction to him? Because now you know what before you only suspected—that one touch, one taste, one embrace won't ever be enough?

No. Absolutely not. Unconsciously sitting up a little straighter, Mallory did her best to dismiss that last idea. If she was hung up on what had happened, it was simply because he'd caught her at a vulnerable moment. Exhausted by another long day, punch-drunk from having eaten her weight in carbohydrates, she'd been feeling relaxed, a little sleepy, almost…happy. And then with a few offhand sentences he'd reduced her to some sort of obligation, demolishing her already mangled pride.

Big surprise that she'd gotten mad. Or that when he'd grabbed her the way he had, all the emotion she'd been holding in the past few months, the fear, frustration, disappointment and loneliness, had simply bubbled up, turned into a soupy sea of lust and swept her away.

Yes, it was beyond mortifying that he'd been the one to put an end to the kiss—and that to do it he'd had to practically peel her off his front.

But so what? She'd endured worse. Hadn't her mother walked out when Mallory was nine to make a new life with a man who didn't want kids? And then there was her darling father, who'd done what he had without a thought to her happiness, much less any concern about what would happen to her when he left.

But that's not Gabe. He does care. That's why he came looking for you, has tried to make your apartment safer, keeps offering to help you out. Isn't a large part of the reason you can't let this go because it rankles that what he seems to care about most is doing the right thing, not you specifically? And that, far more importantly, there's a part of you that still wants to take the easy path, to lean on him and let his broad shoulders carry some of your responsibilities?

Maybe, she answered reluctantly, unwilling to concede there was any truth to what she was thinking, but at the same time unable to dismiss it out of hand.

Yet just the possibility that on some level she wanted to let Gabriel take care of her was alarming. And yet another reason she needed him to keep his distance—which she'd done her best to insure in the note she'd sent him along with the rest of his cash.

And if they did cross paths? She intended to treat him the way she once had—as a distantly amusing acquaintance, nothing more. No matter what he said or did, she intended to smile, make polite conversation and go her own way, her dignity, her virtue, her heart intact.

The reminder steadied her. Suddenly feeling back in control, she refocused her attention on the interview where it belonged. "I worked on the ball for nine years," she said to her former classmate. "Starting in high school."

"Oh, yes, that's right." Nikki nodded as if it was news to her.

"At one time or another, I've headed all of the major committees. Entertainment, venue, refreshments, publicity. I think that gives me a good overview of what needs to be done, when and by whom."

"I suppose it does." The other woman tapped her right index finger against her cheek. "We did make some changes last year, however. I don't believe you were here then, were you?"

"No, I wasn't."

"Didn't you resign from your committee?"

"Yes." Although it wasn't easy, Mallory kept her voice even. "I did." This time last year the first rumors of trouble had started to swirl around her father. Certain that it was all just a mistake, and shocked by how quickly people she'd known her whole life had been to believe the worst, she'd decided to take a break from Denver until he got things straightened out.

Which of course, he never had.

She lifted her chin the merest fraction. "But I've always been a quick study, and I assume that everything I'd need to know is in your former planner's files. And that if I missed anything—" she forced herself to smile "—you or someone else who worked on the event last year would be happy to set me straight."

Nikki sniffed. "You're certainly right about that."

All right, so the conversation didn't exactly seem to be going great. Mallory told herself not to panic. There was still a chance she could turn things around.

Swallowing her pride, she leaned forward. "If you'll just give me an opportunity to show what I can do," she said earnestly, "I promise you won't be sorry, Nikki. I'll work harder than anyone else you might be considering."

The blonde pursed her lips, then suddenly gave the

exasperated sigh of someone forced to perform a truly oppressive task. "I guess you should know that April, the former coordinator, didn't just leave. She was fired."

"Oh." It was a startling piece of news simply because, as far as Mallory knew, it was the only time in the charity event's fifty-five-year history that it had happened.

"'Oh' is right. When she started, we all thought we were so lucky because she seemed so efficient and organized and she kept agreeing to take on tasks that have always been handled by the volunteers. But as we recently discovered, she was in way over her head right from the start, and when things started to pile up, she just set them aside and pretended they didn't exist."

"What sort of things?"

For the first time in the interview Nikki actually looked a little uncomfortable. "Well…there happen to be lots of little items. Deposits and payments that were never sent to various suppliers, an incomplete list of this year's sponsors, and it seems none of the programs or merchant flyers have been put together, much less sent to the printers. Then there's also the fact that at present we don't have anyone contracted to provide the music for the big night."

Mallory considered. While it sounded as if it would be a huge amount of work to get everything back on track, so far none of the obstacles seemed insurmountable.

"There's also a problem with the venue for the fashion show."

"What's that?"

Nikki shrugged. "We don't have one."

Mallory stared at her in disbelief. "But it's always held at the Botanic Gardens."

"Not anymore. Apparently they changed their policy years ago about allowing outside fund-raisers, but we were an exception because Mrs. Wentworth sat on both boards. When her health forced her to step down last year, that changed. Only April didn't bother to mention it."

For once, Nikki was absolutely right, Mallory decided. It was a huge problem since most of the sites that could accommodate such an event—and all of the best ones—would already be booked by other organizations.

Still, if she put her mind to it, she was sure she could come up with a solution. And when she did, it would surely improve her odds of landing a more permanent position in the future.

She took a breath and sat up a little straighter. "I realize it won't be easy," she told Nikki, "but I'm sure I can handle it."

"I take it that means if the job were offered to you, you'd take it?"

"Yes." Mallory sat back and prayed. "Yes, I would."

"Oh, all right then." Nikki shut the file with a snap.

Mallory stared at her in surprise. "Does that mean…I'm hired?"

"I suppose so." The blonde smiled humorlessly at her. "Since the board already agreed the job was yours if you wanted it."

"They did?" She tried to take it in, too stunned to even be mad about Nikki's apparently needless inquisition.

"Yes. Although I'm sure it's only because they've been unable to find anyone else on such short notice. All the really qualified people are working on other projects."

"Right." She'd gotten the job. *She* was Bedazzled's new event coordinator. Between this and cousin Ivan's behest, she could finally start to look toward the future instead of expending all of her energy on just trying to survive.

It was all she could do not to leap up, grab Nikki and dance around the room. Probably not a great idea in light of the other woman's hostility.

"So." Nikki gave an exasperated little huff. "How soon can you start?"

Mallory didn't hesitate. The quicker she got to work, the harder it would be for them to change their mind. "Right now if you'd like."

"I suppose that would be for the best. Since April left, nobody seems to have a clue what anyone else is doing. Of course, you'll have to fill out some paperwork first." She reached out, reopened the file, riffled through it and extracted a handful of papers. She thrust them at Mallory. "Here. It's the standard stuff, W-2, medical and emergency forms. I assume you don't need any help?"

"I think I can manage."

"I'll leave you to it, then." Tossing back her hair, she stood. "When you're done, come and find me and I'll show you your office, get you some keys and a current copy of the event schedule. As you'll see, there are a lot of things on the calendar, starting with a party this weekend out at the O'Keefe's in Lone Tree."

"Thanks." She felt a brief pang about the logistics of getting out to the exclusive neighborhood, then decided she'd worry later. For now she intended to enjoy the moment.

Nikki shrugged. "It's not like it's my choice, Mallory. I'm just doing what I was asked to. If it were up to me, no matter how much we need to fill this position, you wouldn't have been considered, much less chosen. And I'm sure once other people find out you've been hired, they'll feel the same way. Your father cheated a lot of people, and I'm not the only one who hasn't forgotten."

"I'll keep that in mind," Mallory murmured.

"You do that," Nikki said coolly as she sashayed out the door.

Mallory stared after her for a moment, then looked away, giving herself a mental shake. Compared to everything else she'd been through, Nikki's attitude qualified as a minor bump in the road, she told herself firmly. Sure, the injustice of being blamed for dear old dad's misdeeds rankled, and the thought of being thrust back into her social circle in the guise of paid employee was more than a little daunting, but she'd survive. The important thing was that she'd gotten the job.

The reminder brought on a fresh wave of exhilaration. Once more she had to conquer the urge to jump to her feet and twirl around like some giddy little teenager. Still, it was the kind of news that wouldn't feel completely real until she shared it with someone.

She had her purse open and was reaching for her cell phone when she realized that the only person who might actually understand her elation was Gabe.

She snatched back her hand. Good grief! Where had that come from? Because it most certainly wasn't true. And even if it was, he was the last person on earth she'd call since he'd no doubt take it as a sign that despite everything she'd said, she secretly wanted him in her life.

Which she didn't. She couldn't, she told herself firmly, as she picked up a pen and began filling out the first of the forms Nikki had left with her, ignoring the slight squeezing sensation around her heart.

For her own peace of mind, from here on out Mr. Killer Lips Steele had to be just another part of a past she might finally be starting to put behind her.

Gabriel knew by the slight tingle of awareness that slid down his spine the instant Mallory arrived at Saturday night's Bedazzled cocktail party.

Taking a sip of his wine, he finished listening to what the delicate blonde at his side was saying, then lifted his head. Aided by his height, he casually surveyed the crush in Melissa O'Keefe's enormous living room.

He wasn't surprised to see Mallory standing just inside the hall entrance. Tonight her streaky caramel-brown hair was piled on her head in an updo that drew attention to the slenderness of her neck, while her lissome curves were draped in a slim-fitting, silvery-pink sheath that was somehow both restrained and drop-dead sexy.

She looked good enough to eat.

An unfortunate train of thought, he realized, as his body reacted to the image that sprang to mind of her tousled, naked and stretched out for his delectation.

He glanced away. Taking another swallow of his wine, he returned his attention to his companion—and found her watching him with an arrested expression on her classically beautiful face. He raised an eyebrow. "What?"

"I wondered why you offered to be my date tonight," his sister-in-law, Lilah, said. "Now, I know."

He met her astute blue gaze with a steady one of his own. "And if I said I had no idea what you're talking about?"

She smiled. "I wouldn't believe you."

"No?"

She shook her head. "No." Gently rubbing a spot on her very pregnant stomach, she glanced pointedly back toward the doorway. "That *is* Mallory Morgan, isn't it?"

He followed her gaze and saw the subject of their conversation was now talking to two of the charity's founders and most influential board members, the white-haired DeMarco sisters, who also happened to be longtime Steele Security clients. "Yes, it is."

"I thought so. The two of us have been playing phone tag the past several days."

"How come?" Annalise, the older of the elderly

DeMarco sisters, smiled at something Mallory said, while Eleanor, the younger, had a more reserved, wait-and-see look on her face.

"It's a long story, but it boils down to my having volunteered to find a new site for the fashion show we always put on, and her being the new event coordinator. Which, by the way, has caused a small furor all on its own."

Gabe abruptly shifted his gaze back to her. "In what way?"

"Let's just say that several of my fellow volunteers have concerns about her being hired."

"Which are?"

Lilah gave a slight shrug. "Pretty much what you'd expect. Can she be trusted to do the job? Is she really qualified? Are they going to have to hide their purses when she's around?"

"You're kidding about that last one, right?"

"I wish I was. But unfortunately, rich people, like everyone else I suppose, tend to be pretty unforgiving when it comes to their money." She paused to take a sip of her sparkling water. "There's also a lot of speculation about just how she wound up with the job." She tilted her head a fraction and considered him. "Clearly someone with influence vouched for her, but nobody seems to know who."

Gabe shrugged. "Don't look at me. Like I said, I'm just here to enjoy the company of my favorite pregnant sister-in-law."

Something glinted in Lilah's big blue eyes, but

whatever it was she chose not to pursue it. "Don't give me that. We both know that you're really here because Dominic asked you to watch out for me while he's in London."

"Well, sure," he said, promptly stepping into the path of a passerby before the man could inadvertently jostle her. "And what's wrong with that?"

"Absolutely nothing. Except that if he doesn't stop worrying all the time, he'll be in the hospital before I am. And don't pretend you don't think his behavior is a little over-the-top," she went on before he could so much as part his lips to protest. "I talked to Cooper the other day, so I know you've all taken to calling him Dr. Demento behind his back."

Gabe might have smiled if not for the genuine concern he saw on her face. "He'll be fine, Li," he said quietly. "It's just that he's an action-oriented guy, and having a child involves a lot of waiting. Add in that he's wired by nature and training to protect you, yet he sees himself as responsible for you being in this situation in the first place, and I'm not surprised he's acting the way he is."

"Crazed?" she suggested drily.

"Exactly. This is just a suggestion, but you might want to consider trying, just for now, to be a little less self-sufficient." Never much of a drinker since he didn't like feeling even mildly impaired, Gabe exchanged his half-full wineglass for water as a waiter passed by bearing a tray. "Maybe if Dom had more to do, he wouldn't feel so out of control. At least that's the way it used to work when he was a kid. The busier he was, the less trouble he got in."

For a moment she just looked at him, then slowly she nodded. "You know, I hadn't thought of that. Not in that context, anyway. But you may be right. Maybe I've been trying so hard not to worry him, I've made him feel as though I don't need him. And nothing could be further from the truth." She smiled sweetly. "You're actually rather perceptive. For a man."

"Thanks." His own mouth curved up. "I think."

They enjoyed a moment of companionable silence, and then found themselves the center of attention as a changing parade of people came up to exclaim over Lilah's pregnancy, ask about Dom's absence, discuss the recent fluctuations in the weather, the upcoming ball, and even, on two occasions, speculate on whether the new coordinator was up to her job.

It was a good hour before they found themselves alone again, and had a moment to simply watch the crowd around them. Or at least, Lilah did. Gabe found his own gaze drawn unerringly back to Mallory.

She'd moved deeper into the room and was currently standing with an older couple, an interested look on her vividly pretty face at whatever they were saying.

And then, she suddenly turned and looked over at Gabe as if they were connected by some invisible tether, and for an instant it was as if they were the only two people in the world.

The moment didn't last, however, as almost immediately she stiffened. Lifting her chin, she deliberately turned her back on him.

"We went to the same high school, you know," Lilah volunteered quietly beside him. "Taylor Union. Mallory was a few years behind me, but even back then… She had quite a reputation."

He turned to look at her. "For what?"

"Wild behavior. I can't say I paid much attention, but I think I remember something about a midnight horse race that destroyed a fairway out at the Fairlawn Country Club. And I have a very clear memory of Gran and her friends talking during my first spring break from college about how disgraceful it was that Cal Morgan just let her do whatever she wanted. As I recall, she'd flown herself and a handful of friends to Rio for Carnivale. I'm not sure, but I don't think she could have been much more than sixteen."

Gabe tried to imagine it. But he just couldn't. It was about as far from his experience of scrambling to make ends meet and trying to keep the family together while they bounced from one military base to another, as Paris was from Fort Dix. "Sounds like an interesting childhood."

"Does it?" Lilah pursed her pretty lips thoughtfully. "I suppose, growing up the way you did, with so much responsibility, it might."

"But?"

"Oh, I don't know. I just think that's awfully young to have so much freedom and absolutely no rules or guidance." She paused, then sucked in her breath.

"Dear God in heaven," she said with a dismayed groan. "That sounded just like my grandmother."

"Nope," he said emphatically. "Not even close."

Her grateful look prompted them both to laugh.

Sobering, she touched her fingertips to his forearm. "I guess what I mean is… Doesn't it strike you as sort of sad that she didn't have anyone to place restrictions on her, if only for her safety? And make you wonder what kind of parent lets a girl that age go traipsing off to South America without any supervision?"

An egocentric bastard like Cal Morgan, he found himself thinking. But before he could say as much, Lilah suddenly grimaced and pressed a hand to the small of her back. "Uh-oh."

He tensed. "What?" All joking aside, he didn't want to think what Dom would do if anything happened to his wife.

"All the sparkling water I've had tonight just caught up with me," she said serenely, seemingly unaware that she'd just given him a momentary case of cardiac arrest. "If you'll excuse me?" Without waiting for an answer, she pressed her glass into his hand and took off in the direction of the powder room.

Filled with a combination of exasperation, relief and awe—he'd rather face a truckload of terrorists any day than be a pregnant woman—he watched as she made her way across the room and disappeared into the hall, her normally light, graceful walk transformed into something that was anything but by her altered center of gravity.

Then his gaze swung back toward Mallory, only to find that she was gone, too. A quick look around had him homing in on her slim back and taut fanny just as she disappeared out a set of French doors leading out to the terrace.

He was halfway across the room before he'd made a conscious decision to go after her. Keeping to the same brisk pace, he stepped out onto the flagstones of a wide, multilevel patio dotted with huge pots of bright flowers and a dozen wrought iron tables. In sharp contrast to the last time they'd been together, the night was balmy, ripe with the scents of freshly mown grass and incipient spring.

Nodding to several seated acquaintances, he went down the wide, shallow steps to join her at the railing where the patio overlooked the pool.

She turned to glance at him as he walked up and he saw her tense. Okay, it was hardly unexpected given the way they'd last parted, the terse little missive she'd sent him afterward, or the way she'd reacted inside when their gazes had met so briefly.

That was why apologizing was already part of his plan. He'd do whatever he had to do to get them back to the tentative truce they'd briefly enjoyed over dinner the night he'd kissed her.

Not that he expected her to make it easy, he admitted, as she deliberately turned her back to stare out at the pool.

"Well, surprise, surprise," she said. "If it isn't Denver's own Mr. Here, There and Everywhere One Wishes He Wasn't."

"It's nice to see you, too, sweetheart."

"Of course it is." There was the slightest pause, and then she glanced sideways at him. "It's hardly a secret that I'm irresistible." Holding his gaze, she idly began to wind a glossy tendril of hair around her finger.

An untrained observer might have missed the subtle shift in her manner. But not someone for whom the slightest change in a person's inflection could sometimes be the difference between life and death. Curious, he said mildly, "No argument from me there."

"Oh, dear." She turned more fully in his direction, and looked up at him through the dark fringe of her lashes. "How tragic for you. I do hope my fatal allure isn't the reason you're here tonight."

"And why's that?"

"Promise you won't be crushed?"

"I'll try to survive." Of everything he'd anticipated from her—the cold shoulder, outright anger, a flat refusal to acknowledge him at all—a reemergence of her old flirtatiousness hadn't even made the list. But then, as he really should've figured out by now, Mallory was rarely predictable.

But then, neither was he.

"Yes, well, the thing is," she sailed on, "as much as I cherish your unselfish devotion, I'm afraid I'm otherwise engaged this evening."

He raised an eyebrow. "Really?"

"Yes."

"Let me guess. Raoul?"

It took her a moment to get it. When she did, her

eyes narrowed for the merest instant. Almost immediately, however, she recovered. "Ah, yes, Raoul. How I wish I could say yes. But the truth is, the poor darling is still recovering from our latest incredibly athletic encounter. No, I happen to be here in an official capacity. You may not have heard, but I've been hired to take over as Bedazzled's event coordinator."

"As it happens, my sister-in-law did mention that earlier. Congratulations."

"Thanks." It was the perfect place for her to point out yet again that she could take care of herself. Yet true to form for tonight, she took a different tack. "Just who is your sister-in-law?"

"I believe you know her," he said casually. "Stunning blonde, impressively pregnant?"

She straightened. "Lilah Cantrell is your sister-in-law? Since when?"

He felt a stab of satisfaction as she confirmed his hunch that she'd been paying more attention to him tonight than she'd let on. "It's Lilah Cantrell Steele these days. She and Dom celebrated their first anniversary in February."

"Gosh, I guess I missed the wedding. Of course, a year ago… I would've been Down Under for the Sydney Regatta, cheering on those hunky Aussies. Such lovely blokes." She gave a fond little sigh, then cocked her head as if thinking. "No, wait. That was March. In February it would've been New York for fashion week."

She waved her hand dismissively. "In any event, it's

good to know someone was finding true love while I was off being useless and spending pots of money." She flashed a brilliant smile that didn't come close to reaching her eyes.

He reached out instinctively, touching his hand to her shoulder. "Mallory—"

"Oh, look," she said brightly, glancing up toward the house at the same time she moved just out of reach. "Isn't that Lilah now, heading this way? She must be looking for you. And I really must circulate."

"Actually," he interrupted, stepping over and blocking her path so she couldn't leave without dodging inelegantly around him, "I'm sure she's looking for both of us. She mentioned something about needing to talk to you about the fashion show, and I told her I'd find you and arrange it."

"And just how do you propose to do that?" she said, just as Lilah, whom he'd always considered to have impeccable timing, arrived to join them.

"I wondered where you'd disappeared to," his sister-in-law announced, a knowing gleam lighting her eyes in the instant that her gaze met his. "Not that I'm surprised," she went on, turning conspiratorially toward Mallory. "The Steele men simply can't seem to resist smart, beautiful women." She smiled, and her genuine friendliness was impossible to miss. "Hi. I'm Lilah. I'm sure we've been introduced before, but it's nice to finally get to say hello. Particularly after the way we've been missing each other on the phone."

Clearly surprised by the other woman's warmth, after a brief hesitation, Mallory smiled back. "Yes, it is."

"I was just about to suggest," Gabe jumped into the conversation, "that Mallory let us give her a ride home. That way you two will finally have a chance to discuss your business and she won't have to wait for a taxi." He shifted his gaze from Lilah to Mallory. "That is what you're planning, right?"

"Yes, but it's really no problem—"

"Don't be silly," his brother's beautiful wife interjected, her inherent kindness coming to the fore exactly as he'd counted on. "It'll take forever for a cab to get here, if you can get them to come out at all on a Saturday night. Besides—" she sliced him a look that let him know that while she was going along, she knew very well what he was up to "—I'd love a chance to visit. Frankly, there are times when even the nicest man can be a little tiresome."

"Great. It's settled then," Gabe said, judging it to be an excellent time to make himself momentarily scarce. "I'll go get the car while you two say your goodbyes, and meet you out front."

And with that he gave both women a gallant smile and headed inside.

Six

"So I guess you're not speaking to me," Gabe remarked into the silence that filled the SUV.

Staring out at the distant lights as they drove back toward the city after dropping Lilah off at her home in the Denver foothills, Mallory parted her lips to say *that's right*.

Then she caught herself.

No. She'd already been much more gracious than he deserved, chatting with Lilah about the fashion show debacle and exchanging ideas about what they might do about it, just as if she wasn't perfectly aware of how he'd maneuvered her into accepting this ride.

More to the point, it was clearly a trick question. Regardless of what she said, she'd be trapped into defending her answer. And once she did, she knew exactly what would happen.

He'd say something charming or aggravating or arrogant or insightful. What, it didn't matter. And she'd feel angry or enchanted or amused or alarmed, the particulars of which also wouldn't matter.

Because just like back at the party, the whole time they were talking her heart would be racing and her stomach jitter-bugging. Worse, she wouldn't be giving the conversation her complete attention because no matter how hard she tried to concentrate, part of her would be wondering whether a second kiss between them would be as explosive as the first.

Given that she'd already decided there wasn't going to be a second kiss, her continuing fixation on the subject was mystifying. Granted, his unexpected presence at tonight's event had taken her by surprise. And in retrospect, she could see that her decision to resume her old party girl persona with the hope of re-establishing a proper distance between them had been a miscalculation.

She simply should have ignored him. And if that hadn't worked, she should have behaved like the rational adult she was and pointed out that in light of her new job, she clearly didn't need his assistance.

But she hadn't. Instead, she'd gotten sucked into having a conversation with him and look where it had landed her. Once again they were alone in a car in the dark. Only unlike a week ago when she'd so foolishly lowered her defenses, this time around her awareness of him was on heightened alert. She found herself listening intently to his every breath, her pulse jumping each time he moved, her body humming with the effort of remaining aloof.

Even more confounding, there was a reckless part of her that had an alarming desire to slide across the seat, climb into his lap, bury her fingers in his hair and take another taste of that hot, chiseled mouth.

Forget mystifying. It was mortifying. And another excellent reason to remain silent, no matter what.

"Well, if you're not going to talk, I will," Gabe said out of the blue, as if he'd read her mind and decided it wouldn't do for her to think she was actually in control of the situation. "Because I want you to know that I'm sorry about what happened the last time we were together."

Pursing her lips, she forced herself not to react even though she suddenly felt as if he'd jabbed her with a knife. Sure, *she* regretted that kiss, but the idea that *he* might had never even occurred to her.

"Not for kissing you," he went on, just as if he really were clairvoyant. "But for letting you think that my interest in you isn't first and foremost about you as a person. That may not have been the case initially, but it is now, and it's important to me that you know it."

Well…damn. How exactly was she supposed to respond to that? Or, more to the point, how could she not? "I—that's…thank you."

The words seemed woefully inadequate the moment

she said them. Yet the truth—that he'd just slid past her guard and said the one thing she'd wanted to hear before she'd even known it herself—was far more than she was willing to reveal.

"I just thought you should know."

Once again, silence descended. Feeling totally inadequate, thinking there must be something more she could add, Mallory looked out the window, hoping for inspiration. And felt a niggle of surprise instead as she realized that at some point during their conversation they'd left the highway and were now winding through a sprawling community of large, modern homes set well back from the road.

"Where are we?" she asked.

"My place," he answered, turning into a wide, well-lit driveway leading up to a contemporary wood and stone house with, of all things, a basketball hoop attached to the three car garage.

One door of which had started to rise.

"*What?*" She swiveled to face him. "No. Absolutely not, Gabriel. I agreed to a ride, not a tour of your own personal Bat Cave. And if this is what your little declaration was really about, you trying to lull me into thinking you can be trusted—"

"Relax, Mal," he said, a steely note of temper edging into his voice. "I didn't bring you here for sex, if that's what you're thinking." Pulling into the garage's cavernous interior with the ease of long practice, he switched off the car engine and hit the button to lower the door behind them. "Not that I'd say no if you decided you were up for it." Beneath his attempt to smooth things over, something darker lurked in his voice that made her want to squeeze her knees together.

She crossed her arms instead.

"Look," he said, pushing open his door. "The *truth* is that I didn't plan to drive into town tonight, and I've got my brother Deke's dog for the weekend, all right? I need to let him out or he's going to start gnawing on the nearest table leg. So while I'd love for you to come in and see my place, I've got no interest in coercing you into doing anything you're not comfortable with."

"Good," she said intractably. "Then you won't care if I wait here."

One big shoulder hitched in a careless shrug. "Suit yourself. Like I said, I won't be long."

Face set, she watched out of the corner of her eye as he climbed out, yanking his tie loose as he walked with the long loose stride that even now had the power to make her stomach hollow. Reaching an interior door, he switched on an overhead fixture so she wouldn't be in the dark when the automatic lights winked out and disappeared inside.

Well, good! For once he'd done exactly what she wanted. Telling herself it was about time, she gave a huff of satisfaction and crossed her legs, deciding a moment later that she could afford to indulge her curiosity by taking a look around.

She wasn't surprised to see the silver sports car parked in the next space over. Whenever she'd thought about Gabe in the past, she'd pictured him with just such a vehicle, living in a stylish penthouse atop one of the city's higher skyscrapers. Or occupying one of the newer mansions in some upscale neighborhood like Cherry Creek or Country Club.

Yet the car was the only visible symbol of the contained, sophisticated loner she'd thought she knew. While the rest of the garage, she realized, appeared to belong to some athletic suburban soccer dad.

There was a trio of bikes and a pair of kayaks hanging from the rafters, along with enough other sporting equipment from snow skis to hockey skates to scuba tanks that he could stock his own store. There was a lawn mower, what she thought might be a snow-blower, shovels, lawn furniture, a set of barbells, a workbench and a tall red tool chest. Everything was efficiently organized and looked to be well maintained.

Not to mention being more Martha Stewart than James Bond. And yet another glaring example of him not being the man she'd thought he was.

But then, she'd never been the person she'd pretended to be, either.

That's right. You've gone from shallow but daring to hiding out in a parked car because you're afraid you might be feeling something real for a change.

The thought had her rearing back against the seat as if she'd been struck. She wanted in the worst way to deny it, but the longer she sat there, in the looming quiet, alone due to her self-imposed isolation, the more she could see it was true. And that being able to take care of herself financially wouldn't mean a thing if she kept following her old pattern of running away any time she felt the slightest connection to another person.

Taking a deep breath, she got out of the car. Then before she could lose her nerve, she walked over to the door and let herself into the house.

A quick look around showed she was in what appeared to be a combination mudroom and pantry, with high ceilings, a checkerboard floor and gleaming cherrywood cabinets.

Listening, she heard the low murmur of Gabe's voice. She followed the sound, walking into a spacious kitchen with stainless steel appliances, more of the same glossy cabinets, a vast expanse of black granite countertops and a big island with half a dozen large, padded bar stools lined up along one side like buttons on a shirt.

Continuing on, she entered the adjoining family room, which boasted a huge fireplace and a burgundy leather sectional anchored by a stunningly beautiful Oriental rug. Stopping briefly to listen, she gave a faint start as a shaggy canine shape suddenly bounded by on the other side of the sliding-glass doors. Then she followed her ears down a wainscoted hallway and was rewarded by the sight of Gabe in what was clearly his den.

As she'd already surmised, he was on the phone, standing with one hip planted against a mahogany desk the size of a small country. What she hadn't imagined was that he would've shed his jacket and tie, unbuttoned his collar and shoved up his shirtsleeves.

Her mouth foolishly went dry at the sight of his

exposed forearms, which were lightly dusted with black hair and corded with muscle.

"That's great, Jake." His eyebrows knit in a slight, surprised V as he caught sight of her in the wide doorway. "What?" He held up a finger to indicate he'd only be a minute. "Yeah, I'll be sure to tell Cooper. And yeah—" he chuckled "—you're right that he's not going to like it."

The soft sound of his laughter tickled her nerve endings like the lash of a velvet whip, raising goose bumps on her flesh.

It made her wonder what would happen when he finally put his hands on her. Because he would, she realized with sudden insight. Something fundamental had changed between them the day of their encounter at Annabelle's, and as she'd learned at the party tonight, there was no going back, no putting the genie back in the bottle.

Unless something unforseen happened—say a meteor streaked out of the sky and crashed down on one of them—it was only a matter of time before their attraction led to its logical conclusion.

So why wait? Why not put an end to this sexual limbo?

She had to admit there was an undeniable allure in the thought of taking charge, doing the unexpected, making Gabriel feel off balance for a change. Plus it was only sex, which in her experience was overrated and overhyped. They'd come together, do the horizontal tango and then—

What? For a moment she was perplexed to realize she didn't know. And then it occurred to her that was actually the whole point. Once they got the sex out of the way, then they'd see.

Her decision made, she lifted her hands and, one by one, began to pull the pins from her hair, dropping them deliberately onto the carpeted floor. When the last one was out, she combed her fingers through the curly mass, gave her head a gentle shake, and sent the liberated locks tumbling down.

Eight feet away, Gabe suddenly straightened.

She reached back, holding his gaze with her own as she unzipped her dress and slowly pushed it off her shoulders. Wiggling her hips sent it sliding down her body. Naked except for her lavender-colored push-up bra, matching thong and Jimmy Choos with their stiletto heels and peekaboo toes, she stepped clear of the pool of fabric at her feet, raised an eyebrow—and waited.

"Listen, Jake," Gabe said abruptly, "something's come up. I'll call you back tomorrow." Without taking his eyes off of her or waiting for his caller's response, he hung up.

The sound of him dropping the handset into its base seemed very loud in the sudden silence. Yet he didn't say a word, just took his own sweet time looking her over before finally leveling his gaze at her face. "What the hell, Mallory?" His voice was extremely quiet, his eyes intensely green.

She gave a slight shrug. "I thought about what you said."

"Regarding…?"

"Us. Having sex. And I decided yes. I'm up for it. The question is—" she gave him a look from beneath half-lowered lashes "—are you?"

Pushing away from the desk, he padded toward her. "You really need to ask?"

With a thrill of anticipation, she saw that despite his measured step, there was a dull flush beneath the olive-toned skin stretched over his killer cheekbones. She braced, expecting him to do what any other red-blooded male would—push her up against the nearest wall and pick up where they'd left off on that snowy sidewalk a week and a half ago.

Yet she should have known he wasn't prone to acting without thinking. Coming to a halt when a good foot still separated them, he reached out to cup her face, his palm cradling her jaw while his thumb came to rest against her chin. "First—" his shrewd gaze probed her own "—I think you better tell me what brought this on."

"Excuse me?"

Those expressive eyebrows rose. "Ten minutes ago you'd barely talk to me except to say you weren't setting foot in my house. An hour before that I had to practically twist your arm so you'd agree to let me drive you home. But now it seems you're hot to get it on with me. So the real question is—" he tapped the pad of his thumb against her bottom lip "—what's changed, Mallory?"

She gave him her coolest smile, "Didn't anyone ever tell you it's a girl's prerogative to change her mind?"

He just looked at her.

"Oh, all right," she said. "I got to thinking about it and realized this thing between us has been going on for a long time and I thought maybe we'd both feel better if we just went ahead and got it out of the way. Of course, that was back in the last century when I was still deluded enough to think that my stripping naked would be enough to turn you on—"

Thrusting both hands into her hair, he cut her off in midtirade by kissing her.

Except...*kiss* was too tame a word to describe what he was doing with those warm, skilled, sculpted lips. It was a claiming, Mallory thought hazily as his mouth slanted over hers. A possession. Or maybe an instant, overpowering addiction. Reaching up, she curled her fingers into his shirtfront to anchor him in place and parted her lips to accommodate his.

His response was immediate. His tongue breached her mouth, strafing her teeth and the inside of her cheeks, a hot, slick invasion that made her moan. Cupping her shoulders, he reeled her in even closer. His palms kneaded her flesh, while his fingertips skated up and down the outer ridges of her shoulder blades, making her arch like a cat being stroked. The heat from his solid, cotton-covered chest felt delicious against her breasts.

And then, to her shock, he lifted his head and eased back a fraction, dislodging her hands. "What's wrong?" she demanded, struggling to catch her breath.

He gave a slight, husky laugh and she felt her nipples tighten in reaction. "Nothing. Absolutely nothing. Only...why the hurry?" He took a full step back and it was all she could do not to pursue him. "Like you said, this has been a long time coming. We've got the whole night. I want it to be one to remember."

A faint sensation of alarm rippled through her. What she'd envisioned between them when she'd set this in motion had been something down and dirty, hard and fast, a quick union meant to scratch an itch, nothing more. While what he was proposing….

She dampened suddenly dry lips as he circled around behind her. "What…what are you doing?"

She heard a rustle of fabric as his clothes hit the floor, then nothing but the thump of her heart as he bent his head and grazed the ball of her shoulder with his lips.

"What do you think?" Maddeningly refraining from touching her anywhere else, he unhurriedly began to lay a trail of kisses until his mouth found the curve where her shoulder joined her neck.

"But I didn't expect—" She couldn't seem to stop her head from lolling back as he nipped at the tender spot, then soothed the tiny hurt with his tongue. "That is, I thought…" She'd thought they'd go up in flames so fast he'd never find out she wasn't nearly as skillful at this as he was. Except now…with his mouth…doing that…she couldn't seem to think why it should matter.

His hand found her hip. Big and shockingly warm, it slid across her stomach. "What did you think, Mal? That all I'd want is to throw you down and take you right here, right now? Trust me, we'll get to that." His thumb settled gently against the indentation of her navel, drew a lazy circle. "Just…not…yet."

Spreading his fingers, he pressed her back against the solid wall of his body. She bit her lip to suppress a moan as the crinkly hair on his thighs pressed against her bare bottom.

"You've got the most beautiful skin," he murmured into her hair, reaching to cup her lace-covered breast in his palm. "Soft. So damn soft. It used to make me crazy when we'd run into each other at some party and you'd be so close, yet so far out of reach. The whole time we'd be talking I'd think about what it would be like to lay you down, peel off your gown, run my hands all over you."

Heat, liquid and silky, bloomed deep between her thighs. She squirmed, then squirmed some more as he nuzzled the tender, silken seam where her neck met her ear.

"I...I wondered, too." Was that breathless, husky voice really hers? "About us. But I never imagined—"

She broke off as he slowly rubbed his fingertip over her lace-covered nipple and sensation rushed through her, pooling deliciously at her tight, aching center.

She shivered even as a part of her protested it wasn't enough. She wanted to feel his hands on her, experience the touch of those hard palms and slightly calloused fingertips on every inch of her skin.

Her bare, overheated, aching-for-his-touch skin.

"What?" He slid the damp heat of his mouth up to press a kiss to the corner of her lips. "What didn't you imagine?"

She took a long, shuddery breath. "That being with you would make me feel…like this."

Like so much else in her life, in the past her displays of sexual desire had been mostly a pretense, an act she'd put on because it was expected.

But not this time. Not with him. She wanted, she needed, she *ached*, and all with a fervor that was demolishing the very foundation of the walls she'd once depended on to protect herself.

She didn't care. What mattered was the heat from his body blazing against her own, the magic of his mouth at her throat, this unfamiliar craving…for Gabriel. Squeezing her eyes shut, she reached down and managed to release the fastener of her bra. Then she held her breath as he pushed the lacy cups out of his way, covering the soft mounds in his hands as her breasts sprang free.

She moaned at the sheer pleasure of his touch. Then moaned again as he began to shape her sensitive nipples with his thumbs and forefingers. Time dissolved as the stiff little points grew even harder and longer, her need for him stronger.

Desperation started to consume her. She rotated her hips in a mindless attempt to alleviate the ache deep at her core, and felt a thrill of anticipation as she registered the hot, heavy weight of his erection nudging against her. She heard his breath hitch, and she executed another little bump and grind, pouring gasoline on the fire with an instinct she never dreamed she possessed.

"Please," she entreated. "This is… Oh, Gabe, it isn't enough." Turning her head, she pressed hot kisses to the corner of his eye, the top of his cheekbone, the curve of his ear. "I want more. I want you."

"Dammit, Mallory." He no longer sounded the least bit amused. "You're not playing fair."

"Don't you get it?" To her chagrin, her voice trembled the slightest bit. "I'm not playing at all."

He swore. Yet even as his heartfelt profanity sliced through the air, he was whirling her around and sweeping her into his arms.

"What're you doing?" she exclaimed, twining her arms around his neck as he began carrying her down the hallway.

"I want to see you in my bed. God knows, I've pictured you there often enough." Slowing, he bent his head and slanted his mouth over hers in a kiss that was all teeth, tongue and carnal intent.

By the time he straightened, she was dizzy with desire. Burying her face in his throat, she held on tight as he bounded up the wide, curving staircase that punched upward to a second-story gallery.

Not the least out of breath, he crossed a small landing and strode into what was obviously the master suite. As he flipped on a lamp with a thrust of his elbow at the wall switch, she had a quick impression of high ceilings, a stone fireplace and a wide bed covered with a dark glossy spread.

Then he set her on her feet and her surroundings ceased to matter. Her attention was all on his starkly masculine face, with the obvious hunger stamped on his hard mouth and the heat glittering in his heavy-lidded eyes.

And oh, that body. He was all rangy lines and solid muscle, with wide, olive-bronze shoulders, powerfully curved arms and small, flat nipples set in the slope of rock-hard pectoral muscles. Then there was a ripple of washboard abs covered by more taut, golden skin and a shallow dimple of a navel dotting the slash of silky hair that disappeared like an inverted exclamation mark into his briefs.

Briefs that appeared to be strained to the limit by the heavy jut of his cotton-covered sex.

The room suddenly seemed far too hot. And to be lacking something essential. Like air.

"Mallory."

The sound of his voice jerked her gaze to his face. "What?" She took a deep, desperately needed breath.

His eyes, so hot only seconds earlier, were now hooded, his mouth grim. "If you're thinking of calling this off, do it now."

Shocked, she realized he meant it. That despite everything they'd already shared, and the indisputable proof that he was more than ready to finish what she'd started, he'd stop right now and let her walk away if that's what she wished.

Except there was nothing in the world she desired less. Not with this craving for him hazing her brain, this persistent ache deep inside that she was trusting him to alleviate. "Are you crazy?" Tossing back her hair, she drew herself up, trying hard to ignore the fact that she was clad in nothing but her panties and high heels. "I told you what I want. But if *you'd* rather pass, I'll just go gather up my dress and—"

The proud little lift of her chin demolished one more wall in the crumbling fortress of Gabe's control. "The hell you will," he gritted out, taking half a second to peel down his briefs before lifting her off her feet and tumbling her onto the mattress.

This wasn't how it was supposed to happen, he thought a little wildly as he followed her down to feast on the soft, yielding sweetness of her mouth. He shouldn't be so overwhelmed by this driving desire to claim her. Or be burning up with the fevered need to watch her face when he buried himself deep, deep inside her. Not when his plan had been to take it slow, to see to her satisfaction at least once, maybe twice, before even thinking about his own.

Only that wasn't going to happen. She was making him so hot and crazy that if he didn't find a way to reel it back in soon he was afraid he was going to disappoint them both.

Making space for himself between her thighs, he slid down to kiss her throat, the smooth line of her collarbone, the valley between her breasts. Shaping one lush globe in his hand, he paid homage to the soft undercurve, the plump top swell, holding off as long as he could before he finally zeroed in on her thrusting nipples.

"God, you're pretty. All over, but especially here. Your breasts are the perfect size for my hands. While these—" he lashed one stiff, erect tip with the end of his tongue while gently rolling the other between his fingertips "—are the perfect shape for my mouth."

"Gabriel!" Digging her hands into the bedspread, she held on as if her life depended on it as he finally settled his lips over her and sucked.

Lord, she was sweet. Sweet and chock-full of surprises, not at all the woman he'd always thought she was. The nymph, the siren, the worldly sophisticate—it was pretty clear it had all been an act. While this Mallory, his Mallory, had an unexpected vulnerability that satisfied a need in him he hadn't known he possessed.

By the time he raised his head, they were both gasping for air. Pushing up on one arm, he allowed himself a second to look at her, the finely modeled cheekbones, the delicate chin, those breasts, full and round, the rosy nipples wet from his mouth. Then he started to reach for her panties, only to freeze as her lashes fluttered up and her hand gripped his arm.

"Wait." Wetting her lips, she fought for breath. "Let me—I want…" Abandoning speech with a frustrated huff, she simply let go of his arm and let her fingers roam over his chest to explore the tight bead of his nipple, the corded sinew and muscle that ridged his torso. Then her seeking fingertips skated along his hip bone, dipped into his navel.

Brushed slowly against his iron-hard erection.

He jerked, gritting his teeth as that light, uncertain touch alone pushed him closer to the edge. "Mallory—"

Ignoring his strangled warning, she took a deep

breath and closed her hand around him, measuring him with the grip of her palm for the barest instant before her gaze flashed up to meet his. "Wow," she said breathlessly, before once more dampening her lips. "Now, Gabriel. Now, please."

The stark request propelled him right over the edge he'd been dancing on from the second he'd watched her hair come down. Rearing up on his knees, he slid the thong off her body, then wrestled a condom out of the nightstand, swearing at the tremor in his hands as he suited up.

The next second he was settling back into the notch of her thighs, smoothing a hand over her warm, wet center. Finding her slick and ready, he shifted his weight forward, fighting not to just plunge himself inside her as the tightness of her body slowly gave way to his first blunt probing.

His hands clenched against the mattress at the slick, hot squeezing sensation of her body gloving his. "Okay?" he gritted out.

"Oh, yes."

"Good." Pushing deeper and deeper, he lowered his head to kiss the underside of her jaw, the point of her chin, the sweetness of her lips.

Her hands came around him, stroking his sides, his back, flexing against the base of his spine. "Except…"

"What?"

Moaning softly, she shifted restlessly beneath him, her teeth strafing his bottom lip. "I need…I want…"

"What, sweetheart?"

"I want you." Digging her fingernails into his butt, she pushed against him, arching and rocking… "Deeper."

His shoulders bunching, he drove forward. Pulling back, he waited a beat and repeated that hammering stroke, only to freeze for a moment as she made a frantic sound and her hips slammed up.

Her whole body tightened. Then the silky tightness of her sex squeezed around him, gripping his length as she cried his name and to his shock his own climax came roaring up, tearing a harsh sound of disbelief from his throat as it slammed into him without warning.

Pumping his hips, he poured himself into her, his whole body clenching when she gave a second startled cry and came again.

Spent and unaccountably shaken, every muscle in his body went lax. He collapsed against her, driving her into the mattress, where they lay shivering together, fused from cheek to thigh.

When he could finally dredge up the strength, he carefully rolled them onto their sides, not yet ready to give up his place inside her. He let his mind drift for a while, forcing himself not to think but to simply enjoy his own unfamiliar lassitude, the faint scent of Mallory's shampoo, the sluggish return of his muscle control.

Eventually, he opened his eyes. Studying the striking face across from his own, he was struck by how much she'd revealed to him tonight. And how much he had left to learn.

"Gabriel?" she murmured, her voice still raspy with pleasure. "Are you awake?"

He smoothed an errant tendril of hair behind her ear with his finger, one of the few parts of his body that still seemed to be fully functional. "Sure."

She forced her lashes up, although it clearly took an effort. "Can you move? More than your finger?"

"Absolutely." If he wanted to. Which at the moment, he didn't.

"Do you think—would you mind—could you get these darned shoes off my feet? I can't believe I just made love with them on."

Then again… Pushing up on one elbow, he let his gaze take a leisurely stroll down her lithe, slender body to the only thing she still wore, her black-and-pink stiletto heels.

She had more dips and swells than a carnival ride, and like a teenager viewing that first swift drop off the highest point of a roller coaster, the longer he looked, the more his exhaustion faded, replaced by a jolt of pure anticipation.

The effect on his body was immediate and impossible to hide, and made Mallory's eyes suddenly go wide.

"If you insist," he murmured as he moved down to the foot of the bed, slid her shoes from her feet, then reverently placed them on the floor. "Although personally, sweetheart, I think we ought to get these babies bronzed." Wrapping his fingers around her ankles, he eased them over his shoulders.

Then pressing a kiss to the inside of her knee, he took the first step leading them toward the long, thrilling drop he had planned.

Seven

Mallory surfaced slowly.

Stretching languorously on whisper-soft sheets, she gave a sigh of pleasure at the firm resilience of the mattress beneath her and the perfect weight of the silk blanket enveloping her. Just for a moment, she thought she must be back in her own plush bed in the airy bedroom of the house where she'd grown up.

Until she stretched again and the muscles in her thighs protested. Waking more fully, she went stock-still as she registered the unfamiliar tenderness at her core and the events of last night filled her head.

And knew without a single doubt that she was in Gabriel's house, in Gabriel's room. In Gabriel's bed.

Her eyes snapped open. Taking one hurried look around she realized three things.

It was morning.

She was alone.

And she didn't regret one moment of what they'd done last night. Whatever you wanted to call it—and having sex seemed far too bloodless a term to describe the power, the passion, the tenderness she and Gabe had shared—it had opened her eyes to a world she'd never known existed.

Not once in her twenty-eight years had she suspected that she could feel such need, much less inspire it. And that with the right person nothing that brought them pleasure would feel wrong or embarrassing or awkward. Or that afterward she'd feel complete rather than diminished the way she always had before.

It clearly called for a complete overhaul of her naive assumption that one time with Gabe would be enough. Because now that she knew what was possible, she wanted…more.

Much more.

Yet as she stared up at the coffered ceiling overhead, she realized she wasn't sure how that would work, since she'd never had an actual, full-blown affair before.

Although, really… How hard could it be?

The thought brought a foolish little smile to her face. And even that was all right, she decided as she sat up. After all, it was beyond ridiculous to get embarrassed over a mental image when you'd cherished every last moment…and inch…of the reality.

Combing her hair back with her fingers, she tucked the sheet beneath her arms and leaned back against the headboard, looking around with interest.

In the dawn light limning the edges of the large shaded windows, she saw that the bedspread was a rich dark green, not black as she'd thought the night before. The rest of the room also reflected Gabe's taste, from a burnished walnut antique armoire dominating one wall to a large black on white painting above the fireplace, its stark, curving lines proving on closer examination to be the barest outline of a voluptuous nude.

An oversize chair was positioned to one side of the fireplace, a paperback book opened spine up on the table beside it. Her dress and underthings were draped across the matching ottoman, her shoes placed neatly beside it.

The dog, whose name it turned out was Moose, and whose acquaintance she'd made when Gabe had finally remembered to go down and let the animal in last night, was nowhere to be seen.

There was a black nylon carry-on bag parked by the door.

She was considering the implication of the latter when steps sounded on the stairs. Then Gabriel strode in, fully dressed, a cup of coffee in his hand.

His gaze immediately homed in on her. "Good. You're awake." Striding over, he set the cup on the nightstand beside her and sat, the mattress dipping under his weight.

Feeling just the slightest bit self-conscious in light

of the disparity in their attire, she automatically tilted up her chin. "You look nice."

His gaze skimmed her face, her bare throat, the shadow of cleavage showing above the sheet. His green eyes darkened. "So do you." Leaning forward, he anchored his fingers in her hair and claimed her mouth.

God, but the man could kiss, she thought, as his hard lips slanted softly over hers, inciting a riot of feelings. Forgetting to hold on to the sheet, forgetting about everything but him and the sensations he made her feel, she parted her lips and drank him in, a now-familiar tangle of desire starting to twist through her.

Then almost before it started, it was over and he was pulling away. Still cradling her face, he rubbed the pad of his thumb over her lips before finally dropping his hand. "The coffee's for you."

"Thanks." She made no move to take it, just pulled the sheet back up and waited. Even Moose the dog, who hadn't impressed her as being the smartest mutt on the block, would've figured out by now that something was up.

"Look, I hate like hell to do this, but a situation's come up and I have to go out of town."

Well, of course. That explained the bag. As well as the air of edgy energy that surrounded him and the leashed tension he was doing his best to hide. He wasn't on the verge of telling her "it's been nice, now don't let the door hit you in the fanny on your way out." He had business.

Suddenly able to breathe again, she loosened her grip on the sheet. "Where are you going?"

"Belgrade, to meet my brother Dominic. And I'm afraid I have to take off for the airport soon if I'm going to make my flight."

"Oh." She sat up a little straighter. "In that case, you'd better move so I can get dressed—"

He didn't budge. "There's no reason to rush. As a matter of fact—" reaching into his pant's pocket, he extracted a silver ring with a pair of keys on it, along with what looked to be a business card, dropping them next to the coffee mug "—you're more than welcome to stay."

"Excuse me?"

"Between the fridge and the freezer there's plenty to eat, the Jag's got a full tank of gas, and I'll leave my gas card for you in case you need a refill. The way it looks now, the earliest I'll be back will be the end of the week. So why not take advantage and make yourself at home?"

Why not indeed? It would be wonderful, Mallory thought, to spend more than one night in a real bed, to do her laundry without having to go to the laundromat, to have a car to drive instead of a bus to catch. To take an honest-to-God hot shower without running out of water and to sleep without being constantly awakened by people shouting or babies crying.

Except…then what? It was already difficult to transition each day from the affluent world at work to her gritty existence on Lattimer Street. And although there was nothing she'd like better than to move as soon as she could, she was currently deeper in the hole than she'd been when she'd been hired, thanks to the price of taxis and incidentals and because she'd had to invest in some clothes since too little in her wardrobe had been business appropriate.

For the foreseeable future she was going to have to stay where she was. So just how would it feel to live, even briefly, in such safe, comfortable, attractive surroundings, only to have to give them up at somebody else's whim?

Not too great, she imagined. And even if she could find a way to make peace with the situation, what about the truly alarming discovery that she hated the idea of Gabe leaving?

Here she sat, breathing in his scent, her lips still tingling from his kiss, with him so close that his every exhalation tickled against her cheek, and already she was missing him.

It wasn't supposed to be like this. She wasn't supposed to *feel* like this. Last night should have lowered the stakes between them, put her crazy yen for him in perspective, freed her to walk away.

Instead, she wanted to throw her arms around him, drag him back into bed, beg him to stay.

She settled the sheet more securely around her, took a shallow breath. "Thank you, Gabe." To her profound relief, her voice sounded remarkably even and steady. "But I can't."

"Why not?"

Somehow she managed to conjure up a careless

smile. "Honestly? There's a certain crowd at work who already think I shouldn't have been hired. I'm sure they'd really go to town if I showed up driving your car or they found out I was staying at your house. I think it's just better right now if I try to keep a low profile."

She braced, expecting an argument. But to her surprise, although he didn't look happy, after a second he inclined his head a fraction. "All right. Frankly, I think you're worrying about nothing, but it's your decision."

"Gosh." Her smile became genuine. "Gabriel Steele being reasonable. Do you think I could get that in writing?"

His eyes glinted, even as a corner of his mouth kicked up. "Careful, sweetheart. Don't push too hard."

"I wouldn't dream of it."

"Yeah, right." Once more, he leaned in and brushed his mouth over hers. Then he stood. "Don't worry about the dog. Right now he's outside, and if you'll let him in when you leave, Deke should be by around noon to get him. Also, be sure and take the keys, as well as the card, which has my security code written on it." He indicated the items on the nightstand with a thrust of his chin. "That way, if you change your mind, or something comes up, you'll be able to get in."

"All right. Is that it?"

"No." Pausing near the door, he hefted the bag and looked back at her. "I'll see you next week, so take good care of yourself in the meantime, all right?"

Ridiculously, a lump formed in her throat, since she couldn't remember the last time anyone had expressed even polite interest in her welfare. She swallowed, telling herself she was just overtired. "I will. You, too."

"Bet on it." And then he was gone.

"I see you have your nose to the grindstone as usual."

Seated at the desk in her spartan little office at Bedazzled headquarters, Mallory glanced up at the woman standing in her doorway. "Lilah. Hi."

"Do you have a minute to chat?"

She made a phtting sound. "Like you even need to ask? Of course I do." Setting aside her latest to-do list, she got up and came around to move the box of brochures that someone had dumped on her visitor's chair. "Come. Have a seat."

"Thanks. I know it's ridiculous—" the princess-pretty blonde lowered herself down with an appreciative sigh "—since all I've done today is shop for draperies for the baby's room, but getting off my feet for a while sounds heavenly."

Of all the things that had happened to Mallory lately, her burgeoning friendship with Lilah Steele had to be one of the most unexpected. They'd crossed paths occasionally over the years, of course, but had always traveled in different circles and had very different objectives.

Lilah had been raised by her strict, demanding grandmother to have exacting standards and high expectations. Mallory, obviously, had not.

Yet when she'd approached the other woman after their initial talk in Gabe's car ten days ago, about the idea of holding the fashion show at a private home, Lilah had been enthusiastic. Even better, she'd suggested they try to secure Cedar Hill, her grandmother's palatial estate, for the event. The property was one of Denver's largest and most exclusive, and since it had never before been opened to the public, its use would likely garner added interest and publicity.

With insight on Abigail Anson Sommers from Lilah, Mallory had put together a presentation, called on the autocratic old lady and enlisted her cooperation. And ever since, the two younger women had been busy working out details and finding that for all their differences, they just seemed to click.

Now, she looked at her new friend with sympathy and not a little concern. "Still not sleeping well?"

"No. The heartburn is better, but for the past few days Junior here—" she touched a proprietary hand to her pregnant belly "—seems to have decided it's fun to dig his feet into my bladder at bedtime, so I spend most of the night running to the bathroom. But enough about me." A concerned frown knit the blonde's smooth brow. "Did the police have any luck finding whoever was trying to get into your apartment the other night?"

"No. And honestly, I shouldn't even have mentioned it. Most likely it was just kids. Or maybe Mr. Androsky from down the hall. He tends to get trashed the days his pension check shows up and he may have simply confused my place for his." She waved a hand. "Whatever it was, it's over. And except for a few scary moments for me and some pry marks on my door—

which believe me, was hardly a thing of beauty before—no harm was done."

Lilah didn't look convinced, but to Mallory's relief she let it go. "Any word yet from Mrs. Buckingham?"

"Yes! I can't believe I didn't already mention it. She called first thing this morning. Once she got past her amazement that I wasn't in rehab somewhere and that I'd actually managed to hoodwink someone into giving me a real job, she said they'd be happy to help." Since not even Cedar Hill had a place to park several hundred cars, Mallory had contacted the principal at their old high school, Taylor Union, which was only a scant mile away from the mansion, to ask if they could use the school's parking lot. "Not only that, but in exchange for us acknowledging TU on the program, she offered to donate the use of their buses to shuttle people back and forth."

"That's great," Lilah said enthusiastically.

"It's better than great," Mallory countered, flashing a smile. "It's one more thing I can check off my list."

"Well, you can add another. I spoke to Gran yesterday and she suggested we go ahead and hold the after party at Cedar Hill, too."

Mallory sat up straighter. "Really?" Traditionally, there was always a private party to thank the volunteer models after the fashion show, and not having to shift to another site would mean one less thing for her to worry about. "Lilah, that's fabulous! Thank you."

"I didn't do anything."

"Oh, yes, you did. Without you, I doubt your grandmother would have agreed to any of this."

"I'm not so sure about that. She's very impressed with you—and believe me, that's no small feat. But then, even Nikki Volpe and her crowd, who aren't inclined to cut you any slack, acknowledge that you've been working like a dog to get things back on track."

"It really hasn't been that bad. The bulk of the arrangements for the ball itself were well in place when I took over. Mostly it's been a lot of little things that have needed attention."

"Except for the fashion show."

"Except for the fashion show," Mallory agreed, "and with your help even that's coming together. I talked to a supplier in Littleton this morning who can provide us with the runway, chairs and buffet tables. I've ordered the chocolates and champagne, confirmed with Dillon & Diegos regarding the stylists and with Marchant's about the clothes. And I'm scheduled to meet with the man from Scaffoldi's about the tents out at your grandmother's on Friday."

"Good grief," Lilah said with a most unladylike groan. "It's wearing me out just hearing about it. Do you ever sleep?"

Mallory's eyes glinted with good-natured self-mockery. "Darling, please," she scolded in her best uptown voice. "I spent the better part of twenty-eight years on one long vacation. I'm sure I could stay up for a year and not even put a dent in my reserves."

A dimple flashed in Lilah's cheek. "I take that to mean you're as sleep-deprived as I am. Although I know my situation will greatly improve once Dom gets home."

As Lilah had previously explained, Dominic had gone overseas to check on several operations so he wouldn't have to worry about them when it was time for their baby to be born. "He has a talent for relaxing me."

"I just bet he does," Mallory said, amused by the contrast between her friend's demure expression and the anticipatory gleam in her big blue eyes. "Any word on when that will be?" she asked, reaching for her to-do list.

"Yes, actually. He called this morning and he should be home by Sunday."

"That's great."

"Yes, it is." There was a brief silence during which Lilah considered her knowingly. "It's all right to ask, you know. About Gabe."

She picked up her pen, staunchly ignoring the way her pulse leaped at the mere mention of that name. "What about him?"

"Apparently there was some sort of security breach at the Makedonska Museum that required his expertise, which is why he went to Belgrade. But since they've about got things wrapped up, he should be coming home this weekend, too."

"Well, good for him." She made a quick notation to ask the tent man if he supplied his own electrician, and tried to tell herself that the sudden cartwheeling of her stomach was just a delayed reaction to drinking too much coffee.

After all, Gabriel's longer-than-expected absence had proved to be a good thing, allowing her to focus solely on her job. She'd devoted every waking hour of the past ten days to putting Bedazzled's business back in order, and as Lilah had mentioned, it was starting to pay off.

And even if the thought of seeing him again did make her feel a little nervous and unsettled, well, she supposed that was only to be expected. The single night they'd spent together had shown her a whole different side of him. And of herself.

"I'm sure he's more than ready to get back," Lilah observed. "Although I, for one, am going to miss seeing what new clever thing he can come up with to give you. And I'm not the only one. Your little surprises have been the talk of the office."

Her hand went still. Her first "little surprise," a beautiful but functional briefcase, had been delivered the day after he'd left, with a small, unsigned note that she'd known was from him since it had read, "Bronzed those shoes yet?"

In the time since, she'd received a bottle of her favorite scented hand lotion, a new bus pass, an exquisite lithophane night-light, a Starbucks gift card, a bouquet of lilacs in a lovely little china bowl and a small foam cooler packed with a dozen precooked entrees from one of Denver's best restaurants.

Although none of the items had been terribly expensive, it was obvious some real thought had gone into the selections, and that meant more to her than anything else. Never before had a man cared enough about her to actually spend time—did she dare to say the word?—*wooing* her. It made her feel special, cherished, as if she actually mattered.

It was also absolutely terrifying, since now every time she thought of him she felt a little more of her defenses slipping away.

Setting down the pen, she looked at Lilah. She hadn't said a word to anyone about the gift giver's identity, which meant there was no way the other woman could know it was Gabe for sure. Unless, of course, Gabe had confided in Dom.

Yet even if he hadn't, even if Lilah's comment was pure speculation, she wasn't going to lie about it. Their growing friendship was much too important to jeopardize with a lie. Plus it would be a relief to have it out in the open, to perhaps even confide some of her confusion about what she was feeling to another woman.

She set down the pen, pushed her list away. "How long have you known they were from him?" She wouldn't swear by it, but she thought her friend's slim shoulders relaxed a fraction.

"I was pretty sure right from the start," Lilah admitted.

"Oh. I guess that means he sends gifts to women on a regular basis." And the idea didn't fill her with disappointment. It *didn't*.

"No. Truthfully, I don't think I've ever known him to pay another woman this sort of attention. Usually it's just the opposite. Women are constantly throwing themselves at him."

"Then how—"

Lilah gave a slight shrug and smiled. "I've seen the two of you together. And I've seen the way he looks at you when he doesn't think anyone else is watching. Plus until your flowers came in it, that pretty little bowl used to decorate a shelf in his office."

"Oh." It was silly, but the idea that he'd actually given her one of his belongings was mildly alarming, for reasons she wasn't ready to think about. "Does everyone know?"

"I don't see how. I certainly haven't said a word."

She blew out a breath. "Good."

"But why the secrecy, if I might ask?"

"Of course you can. I wasn't trying to be secretive. Just …private. This is all so new—the job, our…relationship, me actually caring about more than the forecast for spring skiing in the Alps or whether I should wait for Mr. Kenneth to make up with his boyfriend before I let him near my hair with his scissors. For once in my life, I didn't want everyone talking about my business."

Lilah nodded. "Makes sense."

"Also… I don't know. At first, everything seemed so straightforward. My need to feel strong and independent versus Gabe seeing me as some loose end leftover from the mess with my dad that he needed to tie up. But now…"

She trailed off, only to have Lilah unexpectedly finish her sentence. "But now you think there's more to his feelings than that."

"Yes. I do." Just hearing herself say the words made her feel panicky and elated all at once.

"I'm sure you're right. And I'll tell you why."

Tipping her head to one side, she said, "Just how much do you know about Gabe's background?"

Mallory thought about it. "Pretty much what everyone does, I guess. That he comes from a military family, that he's the oldest of a bunch of brothers, that his business is a huge success and everyone seems to respect him."

"That's all true, as far as it goes. But what you need to know if you're going to have a chance of understanding him is that when he was fourteen he lost his mother in a car accident. Jake, the baby of the family, wasn't quite two, with the other seven boys ranging in age between them. As Dom tells it, their dad, an army mechanic who was the big, strong silent type, just lost it. Oh, he provided for the family financially—what he didn't drink away at the base bar. But other than that, the boys were on their own.

"I think they all would've wound up in foster care if not for Gabriel. They were all pretty traumatized, but he stepped up, made sure they had clean clothes and enough to eat, oversaw homework and bedtimes, arranged for day care and doctor's appointments, pretty much took on the role of parent. Eli once told me that it was Gabe, not their father, who got up in the night to comfort him and the others when they had bad dreams or cried for their mother.

"Through it all, he did well in school, always had at least a part-time job. Eventually, he went to the local college on an ROTC scholarship, although he was still essentially raising the younger boys. Then their dad unexpectedly remarried, and he was finally able to throw himself into the military career he'd always wanted.

"Dom says he was burning his way up the ranks, doing special operations work overseas, when their father's second marriage broke up and Steele Senior suddenly announced he was retiring to the Philippines. Gabe felt he didn't have a choice but to resign his commission and come home so he could provide a stable, financially secure home for the youngest boys, Josh, Eli, Jake and Jordan."

Absentmindedly Lilah pressed a hand to the small of her back and shifted in her chair. "Not too surprisingly, his brothers are convinced he walks on water even though they're the first to point out that he can be relentless when he thinks something should be done that hasn't been.

"I guess what I'm trying to say is that he's not someone who takes things lightly, Mallory. When he cares, he cares deeply and when he commits to something, he sees it through. But having said that, as far as I know, he's never opened himself up to anyone but family. Certainly not a woman. So just…be careful with your heart, okay?"

Busy trying to sort through everything she'd just heard, it took Mallory a moment before Lilah's last statement sank in. When it did, she momentarily forgot her tangled feelings regarding Gabriel, surprised that Lilah would be concerned for her.

"I… Thanks," she said awkwardly. She fell silent, and

then, because she was afraid she was making more of the other woman's caution than she should, she reverted to humor. "Although I don't think you need to worry," she said lightly. "Just ask Nikki, and she'll be glad to tell you that we Morgans don't have hearts to hurt."

"Right," Lilah replied. "Like I'm going to be influenced by a woman who told me just two days ago about her plan to end world hunger by getting rich people everywhere to save their leftovers? Please."

Mallory gave a snort of disbelief. "You're not serious."

"Oh yes, I am. And the really sad part is, even though she has all the sensitivity of a rock, just thinking about food is enough to make me hungry these days. So what do you think?" Climbing to her feet, the blonde slid her purse onto her shoulder and looked hopefully at Mallory. "Do you have time for lunch?"

"Considering its noon, and I've been here since six? Yes. Besides, I can always eat."

As for Gabe… As she followed Lilah out the door, she promised herself that unsettling or not, she would think about him later.

Eight

After seventeen grueling hours of travel, Gabe had every intention of going home, taking a long shower and getting a good night's sleep in his own bed. What's more, after nearly two weeks of his brother Dominic's constant company, he planned to do all those things alone.

So how he wound up standing rumpled and jet-lagged in the deserted hallway outside Mallory's Bedazzled office Friday evening was beyond him.

Unless it had something to do with the fierce anticipation that raced through his veins at the sight of her. Not yet aware of his presence, she sat engrossed in something on her computer. Despite the lateness of the hour she looked fresh and professional in a pale yellow wrap dress that brought out the sunny streaks in the curling mass of her hair.

Damned if he didn't want to stride in, scoop her up, lay her down and—

"Are you going to say hello?" she inquired, eyes still riveted to the lighted screen. "Or are you just going to stand there and stare at me?"

He felt a stab of surprise. Then he felt profoundly pleased—and maybe a little relieved—that she also felt this powerful connection. "I haven't made up my mind." He took the first step through the doorway. "It's a helluva pretty view."

"You're such a sweet-talker." Despite the lightness of her voice, her hands resting on the keyboard had begun to tremble. The next instant she was on her feet, starting around the desk as if to meet him halfway, only to stop, draw herself up, seemingly rein herself in. "I— How was your trip?"

"Long." Ever since his brother Jake had gone away to college, he'd considered being able to just pick up and go anywhere in the world at the drop of a hat one of the real perks of his job.

He never tired of seeing different locales, of immersing himself in other cultures, of pitting himself against whatever tried to come after a Steele Security client. The instant he'd go wheels up out of Denver, his focus would zero in on the task at hand, and there it would stay until the problem had been satisfactorily dealt with.

Until Belgrade. Where, no matter how hard he'd tried—and he'd given it one hell of a herculean effort—he'd been unable to banish Mallory from his mind.

She started to twine her fingers together, then caught herself. "When did you get back?"

He ordered himself to be patient, to give her a second to get used to his sudden presence, even though it was taking more willpower than it should have for him to hang back. "About an hour ago. We got lucky and were able to catch a flight a few days ahead of schedule."

"You haven't been home yet?"

"No. There was something I needed to get first."

Her eyes sparked with an emotion he couldn't identify. "What's that?"

"What do you think?" Abruptly, he'd had enough. Forbearance was all very nice, but… Erasing the distance between them, he pulled her into his embrace, something taut inside him relaxing as she made a sound midway between relief and pleasure and locked her arms around his waist.

He wasn't sure how long they stood there holding each other, his face buried in her hair, her cheek pressed to his throat. A little uneasily, it occurred to him that what he'd thought he wanted was sex, yet this simple embrace was fulfilling an equally compelling need.

"So how are you?" he said when he finally lifted his head.

She gave him one last squeeze, then leaned back and smiled up at him. "Great. Absolutely great."

"You better be careful, Mal, or I'm going to think you missed me."

"Well, maybe I did. A little."

The admission pleased him. Perhaps too much.

"So." She reached up, toyed with the open collar of his dark gray shirt. "How did you know I'd be here instead of at my apartment?"

He shrugged. "When I couldn't get you on your cell, I called Stan."

"Who's Stan?"

"He's the night security guy for this building. Both he and Rich, the day guy, moonlight for me when I need an extra pair of eyes or ears. I asked him to check the building log and he confirmed you were still here."

"And let you in."

He nodded. "He knows I can be trusted."

"How deluded of him."

His mouth twitched. "Does that mean there's no way I can convince you to come home with me?" That hadn't been part of his plan, either. When he'd realized he intended to see her tonight, he'd been sure he'd find that he'd exaggerated his desire to be close to her.

Clearly that wasn't the case.

"I wouldn't say that." She gave him a look that he felt in the pit of his stomach. "Although actions do speak louder than words…"

"Amen to that." He bent his head, felt her lashes tickle against his face as he skimmed his lips over her temple and along her jawline. He kissed the sleek softness of her throat, lingered there until he felt her melt against him, found her mouth. Their lips met and clung, and he let himself sink into her, driven by the grinding need for the taste and scent and feel of her that had been building in him almost from the minute he'd walked away from her thirteen days earlier.

By the time he eased back to rest his forehead against hers, her hands weren't the only ones that were shaking. Less than thrilled with the discovery, he put a quick stop to it, assuring himself it was simply an outgrowth of being tired. "How'd I do?"

"How 'bout I tell you when I get my mind back?"

The words and her breathy delivery went a long way toward restoring his equanimity. "I take it that's a yes?" He rubbed a circle on the small of her back. "You'll come to my place?"

"I'd heard that you were quick."

"Smart-mouth. Let's get your stuff and go then."

Stepping quickly around her desk, she shut down her computer and picked up her purse. "I'll need to stop by my place and pack a few things."

"No problem." Hustling her out the door, he clicked off the overhead lights.

Minutes later they were in his SUV and on their way. "Nice night," he observed, savoring the dry balmy air against his face.

"How was the weather in Belgrade?"

"Okay. Humid compared to here. How's your job going?"

"Well, I don't think you'll find my picture in the dictionary next to indispensable quite yet, but I'm working on it."

"Maybe working too hard, if tonight's an example."

She gave a throaty chuckle. "Hearing that phrase applied to me has to be a first. It's also sort of ironic considering the source, who—correct me if I'm wrong—just came off at least a hundred-hour work-week."

"Yeah, well—"

"Don't you dare say that's different," she warned lightly. "The only thing different is that you've been working for years and I've been doing it about ten minutes. Besides, I found out just this morning that there's an office pool on how long it's going to be before I throw in the towel, and I sort of lost my head and bet a hundred dollars on never. So now I can't afford to do anything but see this through."

"Like there was ever any question of that," he said with a snort.

She was momentarily silent, then reached over and squeezed his thigh. "Thanks," she said softly. "That's got to be one of the nicest things anyone's ever said to me."

"It's the truth."

"Yes, well, it means a lot, coming from you. Which reminds me." She twisted toward him on the seat as they slowed for a red light. "I also need to thank you for the wonderful presents. I can't…you really shouldn't have, but honestly, I love every single one."

He glanced over at her and saw to his gratification the unguarded pleasure on her face. Truth to tell, the first item, the briefcase, he'd bought purely on impulse while cooling his heels at the airport. The instant he'd seen it, run a hand over the buttery leather and taken a moment to appreciate its clever but elegant design, he'd known she had to have it.

Then, when he'd realized how much he enjoyed picturing her surprise when she received it, he'd been hooked on the idea of doing more, driven by a need to make her feel special—maybe even a little cherished—that he didn't entirely understand.

Still, seeing the quiet glow on her face, it occurred to him that a subtle change seemed to have taken place in their relationship. That she might actually be starting to trust him just a little.

The realization brought satisfaction…and a razor-sharp prick of concern regarding the future.

"That's odd," Mallory said suddenly.

Shooting a glance her way, he frowned at the perplexed expression on her face as they approached the ramshackle old building she called home. "What's odd?" he asked as he drove past the structure, pulling in at the only available spot at the curb a few doors down.

"My apartment's dark."

"Shouldn't it be?"

"No. I always turn on the small lamp by the sofa when I leave. In case I'm late like this. I guess I must've forgotten to switch it on this morning. Either that or—" her keys in hand, she gave a slight, dismissive shrug and reached for her door handle "—the bulb burned out."

"You're probably right," Gabe said at the same time that he caught her by the arm, tugged her around, plucked away the keys. "But on the off chance you're not, you're going to stay right here."

"While you do what?"

"Go check things out." He retrieved the Maglite from the glove compartment and snapped it onto his belt. "In the meantime—" he raised a hand to forestall the protest he could see forming on her lips "—I want you to be sure to lock the doors behind me when I leave. And promise me that you will not, under any circumstance, set foot from this car." He leveled a look at her that had once set toughened soldiers quaking in their combat boots.

"Or what?" she shot back, completely unfazed.

As was often the case with her, he wasn't sure whether to swear or laugh. "Or I'll be worrying about you instead of paying attention to a potentially dangerous situation."

"Dear God." Her gaze locked on his face, she worried her bottom lip for a second, then stopped and squared her shoulders. "All right. I promise. As long as you swear you'll be careful. And understand accept that if you're not back in five minutes, I'm calling 9-1-1."

"I'm always careful." He leaned forward and gave her a fast, hard kiss on the mouth. "Plus I'm trained for this, remember? And chances are good I'll be back in less than a minute with nothing to report."

"Famous last words," she murmured as he climbed out.

He waited a second, gave a quick nod of approval as

he heard the door locks engage. Then he blanked his mind of everything but his current objective and headed inside.

Whoever had broken into her apartment was long gone by the time Gabe walked in to find her door hanging by a single hinge.

That, however, was where the good news ended, Mallory reflected, as he ushered her into his house hours later.

Apparently angered that she'd had nothing worth stealing, the intruder or intruders had thoroughly trashed her place. Her sofa and bedding had been slashed, the sparse contents of her kitchen cabinets dumped onto the floor, her lamps smashed and the Goodwill tables she'd been so proud of reduced to kindling.

Far more upsetting, someone had taken the time to paw through her underthings, lay them out around the room.

While everyone from Gabe to the police to the apartment manager agreed the destruction looked to be the work of teenagers, Mallory feared she'd been violated by someone who knew exactly what he was doing. That made her feel sick—and wonder if she'd ever find the courage to live in the apartment again.

She was doing her best to hide the tumult churning inside her, however. It didn't seem fair to do otherwise, to reward Gabe's kindness and his steadfast support with tears or a hysterical outburst.

Yet it appeared she wasn't doing as good a job hiding her feelings as she thought when he switched on the lights in his bedroom and frowned, taking a good, hard look at her face. "You okay?"

She dredged up a smile. "I'm fine. Although I'm betting you can't say the same. I think this comes under the heading of be careful what you wish for."

Drawing her deeper into the room, he set down the bag she'd hurriedly packed by the ottoman. "How's that?"

"Isn't it obvious? You ask me to spend the night, and now you're stuck with me."

"Is that what you think?"

She shrugged. "Honestly, Gabe, you don't need to worry. I'm not sure when I'll be ready to go back to my place. But until I am, I have a little money set aside, enough to rent a room somewhere. First thing in the morning I'll start looking—"

"Screw that."

"What?" She couldn't have heard that right.

"Maybe I want to be stuck," he said flatly. "God knows, I'm tired of worrying about you all the time."

Her spine stiffened. "I thought we settled that. I'm not your responsibility."

"No, you're not. But that doesn't mean I don't care what happens to you, dammit."

If for an instant he looked a little taken aback at the forcefulness of his admission, Mallory barely noticed. She was too busy trying to breathe as his words kicked a major support out from under her defenses.

"I admit it made me feel a little crazy to find out that someone's been sniffing around your door," he informed her, pacing over to the window. "And when

I think about what could've happened if you'd been home when the bastards broke in, it scares the hell out of me. But it's just because I want you to be safe, Mal. If that's a crime, you may as well convict me now, because it's not going to change."

He'd actually been frightened? For her? The one person on earth she thought of as totally fearless? Her throat went tight. "Gabriel—"

"As far as finding somewhere to stay," he steamrollered on, "if paying your own way means that much to you, then fine—rent a room from me. I've got three that are empty. Although I wish like hell you'd just agree to share the one we're standing in."

"All right." She swallowed. "I will. I do."

"What?"

"If you want to be my landlord, at least temporarily, okay." It would only be until she figured out where she went from here, she promised herself. "But do you think…could we discuss it later?" To her mortification, reaction was finally beginning to set in and her voice was starting to shake. "Right now, would you m-mind terribly—could you just hold me? Please?"

He was across the room and scooping her up before the last word was completely out of her mouth. With a sigh of relief, she looped her arms around his strong, warm neck and let him carry her over to the bed, where he sat and scooted back against the headboard with her across his lap.

"I'm sorry. I don't mean to be such a baby." Except that she did. It was undeniably sweet to be able to lean on someone else—on him—if just for a moment. Burying her face in his shoulder, she closed her eyes, soaking up the heat that seemed to roll off him and radiate right down to her bones, displacing the chill that up until then she'd thought might never go away.

"I keep thinking about what might have happened, too," she admitted. "And the thought of somebody touching my personal things totally creeps me out. And then, for you to say you care…" Her breath shuddered out. "Nobody's ever cared before…."

"Shh." Rubbing his hand over her back, he began to rock her in the universal motion of comfort she'd experienced rarely in her life. "Easy, baby. You've been through a lot tonight, but you're okay now. I didn't mean to upset you."

"Oh, you didn't," she protested. "Not the way you mean." Listening to the steady beat of his heart beneath her ear, feeling the strength of the hard, lean body supporting her own, it dawned on her that she felt safe for the first time in months—maybe years.

For a second the irony of it stole her breath. That the one man on earth she'd always considered a threat to her peace of mind was now the one person she trusted…

It was the most unexpected gift of all. And it made her want to give back something equally important. Yet the only thing of value she had—even it was questionable—was a small measure of truth about herself.

She drew in a breath, forced herself to relax her hold on him enough that she could lean back, face him when she spoke.

"I wasn't exactly up-front with you in the beginning, about being broke," she said quietly. "I *was* irresponsible, and I did recklessly spend too much money, but… My father didn't just steal from all those investors, Gabe. He cleaned out my trust fund, too."

He stiffened. "Jesus, Mal. Why the hell didn't you tell me?"

"Because it was nobody's business but my own. And I—" She hesitated, finding the next words even harder to say than she'd imagined. "I was ashamed that he would do that to me. I mean, I always knew I was low on his priority list. Somewhere above him having a faultless manicure but below whoever he was currently sleeping with. As a kid, I did everything I could to get his attention, pulling stunts that always got everyone who participated but me grounded for life, while my dad—he barely noticed."

She sighed, slid her fingers into the open V at the top of his shirt, needing that contact with his warm smooth skin even as she realized the words were starting to come a little easier.

"I think that's when I finally accepted it was no use. And decided that if he wasn't going to care, neither was I—about him, about me, about anything. I was just going to have fun. So when he disappeared, it was a really rude surprise to discover how much it hurt. And then to find out he'd stolen my trust money…"

"That selfish sonofabitch." Just for a second, before he could mask it, he looked utterly menacing. Then to her complete surprise, he gathered her close once again.

Despite the gentleness of his embrace, she could feel the tension thrumming through him. "If I'd had the slightest clue—" He broke off, but the grimness of his voice said it all.

"It wouldn't have made any difference. Because it wasn't just his fault. Up until he took off, I was just phoning my life in, not paying attention. And then, when I realized what he'd done, what I'd allowed him to do by being so careless with my own affairs, I felt so incredibly stupid. I'm ashamed to admit it, but I wasn't sure what to do, so for a while I didn't do anything and that just made everything worse."

He gently stroked his hand over her hair. "You were in shock."

"Maybe." She blew out a breath. "Mostly I was just clueless. It took getting evicted from the house, then having the hotel where I'd gone to stay throw me out, for me to realize that if I wanted to survive, I was going to have to take care of myself. And because I wanted to do it right, start off with a clean slate, I promptly sold off the only thing of real value I had left, my grandmother's jewelry, and paid off all my debts, thinking it was the honorable thing to do. Of course, in hindsight I can see that not leaving myself a cushion—on the off chance that I couldn't find a job that paid enough to live on—was a mistake, too.

"I guess what matters—" she tipped back her head, looked at him "—is that I don't ever want to feel that way again, Gabe. As if I'm not smart enough or competent enough to run my own life."

Inexplicably, something dark and unsettled flashed through his gloriously green eyes. "Mallory, you're none of those things."

"Maybe not now, but I was. Which is why I can't tell you how much your backing off, not pressing me all the time to do things your way, means to me."

"Mallory—"

"No. Don't." She pressed a finger to his mouth. "You don't have to say anything. Just…I need you, Gabriel. Make love with me."

She felt him jerk at her words. Moved—and amazed—that she could affect him so, she shifted in his arms, brushing her lips over the silky strip of skin behind his ear, the outer edge of his eye and down along the elegant line of his cheekbone until she finally reached his mouth.

His hard, beautiful, indisputably male mouth.

Sliding her hands into his cool, slippery hair, she tipped her head and softly, softly molded her lips to his.

The kiss was exquisite. A sweet meeting of need, an exchange of comfort, an acknowledgment of barriers tumbling down. Nestled together, time slowed as they savored each other, exploring the bow of an upper lip, touching tongue to tongue, feasting on a plump bottom curve, teeth gently shaping moist, tender flesh.

It was like mainlining champagne, and with every sip, every nip, every caress of tongues Mallory felt her distress over the break-in, her uncertainty about the future, her sorrow over her father, fading away.

The only thing that mattered was Gabriel. His taste

on her lips, his scent filling her head, his elegant hands trailing fire over her skin.

Shoes hit the floor, clothing was peeled off, underthings stripped away and discarded. Murmuring his name as they knelt, facing each other in the middle of the big bed, Mallory was bombarded by sensations as they continued to kiss.

There was the slippery coolness of the comforter against her knees and the tops of her feet. The satiny tickle of her hair trailing over her back and shoulders. And Gabe, all warm, powerful muscle and lean angles, his hands cradling the small of her back, his chest abrading her tender nipples as they swayed together, mouths still fused.

The were like two perfectly matched puzzle pieces, she thought hazily.

Moved by a need larger than herself, she opened her eyes, driven to consider Gabriel's strong, compelling face, to admire the slash of his eyebrows and to-die-for cheekbones, his straight nose and tough but sensitive mouth. And as she looked, she felt something fundamental inside her change.

As if sensing her scrutiny, Gabe raised his dense black eyelashes to lock his glittering gaze on her own. "Are you all right?"

"I'm great."

A faint smile curved his mouth. Lowering his head, he kissed the underside of her jaw, the tops of her shoulders, the notch of her collarbone.

"Before, I didn't know—" her voice wobbled as his

head dipped lower and he closed his mouth over one straining nipple "—I could feel this way. That it was possible to want…the way I want you."

For a bare instant, he went still. And then, as if he'd been holding it in, he said fiercely, "Good. Because you're mine, Mal. *Mine*." He raked his teeth over her, a low proprietary growl issuing from his throat. Then he sealed his lips around and sucked. Hard.

The breath exploded from her lungs and she arched, only the support of his hands keeping her upright as she shuddered from the pleasure of his touch—and from his unexpected words, which fulfilled some primitive, unexpected need to be claimed she hadn't known she possessed.

But she did need—she needed him. That became crystal clear as he lowered her onto her back and knelt between her parted thighs. Sliding his hands beneath her bottom, he bent down and trailed his lips over her midriff, pausing to dip his tongue into her navel.

He nuzzled the satiny skin of her abdomen and she felt a shivering excitement. It was matched by growing anticipation as his mouth began to trail lower and lower. "Gabe—"

Her mind seemed to blank and her entire focus to zero in on his slightest movement as he slid the pad of his fingertip along the aching cleft of her sex, and into the silky heat inside. "You're beautiful. So soft, so ready… So wet. You make me crazy, Mal…"

Settling his mouth against her there, he kissed her, deep and intimately, the flick of his tongue startling a cry from her and sending her heels digging into the mattress.

Caught between the upward thrust of the arm braced beneath her, the slow advance and retreat of his broad, marauding finger, the steadily increasing suction of his mouth, Mallory gave herself over to his power. Pleasure built, slow and steady, at first dancing along every sensitized nerve ending, then slowly coalescing into the single, throbbing point between her legs. Robbed of speech, forgetting to breath, she strained against him, wanting, wanting….

Him. Just him.

Forever him.

The realization, along with the rapid, repeated stab of his tongue, sent her spinning and she came apart like a house of cards in a high wind. "Oh. Oh. *Oh*. Gabriel!"

The last syllable of his name was still hanging in the air as he came rocketing up and caught her close. His hands biting into her hips, he thrust himself inside her, big, hard and hot, his sudden, unexpected possession detonating another, even stronger ripple of pleasure. She wrapped her arms around him, meeting him thrust for heavy thrust while that second orgasm began to roll through her. "Don't stop, don't stop, don't, don't, don't—"

His mouth found hers, caressing, demanding, giving. Feeling as if she were riding the crest of an unstoppable wave, Mallory held on tight as he drove her higher and higher, until suddenly something inside her gave way. Caught by a profound punch of pleasure, she cried out, then cried out again as Gabe's big body began to quake and she heard him call out her name as he came.

Breath sawing harshly in and out of oxygen-starved lungs, they sank bonelessly into the mattress, holding tight to each other. It was a good while later when they finally managed to wrestle back the covers and slide between the sheets. Bunching a pillow under his head, Gabe settled her against him, leaning down to press a kiss to her temple as she nestled close, her cheek against his chest.

"Mal?" Yawning, he smoothed a hand over her shoulder.

"Hmm?"

"I'm sorry about the circumstances, but I'm glad you're here."

There seemed no way to respond to that with anything less than honesty. "Me, too."

"As for the rest of it, don't worry. We'll figure it out."

We. She told herself his automatic assumption that he'd be part of some future discussion should have alarmed her. Yet as she felt him settle a little farther into the bed, heard his breathing deepen as twenty-four hours without sleep and his trip across numerous time zones finally caught up with him, she decided that just for tonight, she could let it go.

There'd be plenty of time tomorrow to reestablish some boundaries. Right now, however, there was no place she'd rather be than lying here with Gabe in the dark, safe in the warm circle of his sheltering arms.

Because oh, dear Lord. Somewhere along the line she'd foolishly gone and fallen in love with him.

Nine

"Correct me if I'm wrong," Mallory said, making no attempt to hide her glee as the basketball Gabe had just launched at the hoop in his driveway hit the rim, teetered for an instant, then bounced back to the ground without going in, "but I believe you just added an *E* to H-O-R-S-E. Which means I win." She smiled triumphantly. "Again."

Propping his hands on his hips, Gabe shook his head and did his best to look disgruntled. It was damn hard to pull off, however, while she was standing there looking so pleased with herself.

With her face glowing, her hair drawn up in a ponytail and her slim, leggy figure displayed by a pale pink velour jogging suit almost as soft to the touch as her skin, she looked quintessentially female—soft, silky, seemingly too delicate to lift more than a pompom. Yet she'd just taken him two times out of three at the old match-me-if-you-can hoops game, a feat he'd never hear the end of if his brothers got wind of it.

And he didn't give a damn.

He'd never spent this kind of concentrated time with a woman before. Hell, prior to Mallory, he'd never even invited one to stay overnight at his house. After growing up in a big family, his time spent in the military, and then the past few years riding herd on his rowdy younger brothers, he'd become fiercely protective of his privacy.

Yet with Mallory it was different. Granted, she'd been there hardly more than a week. And it wasn't as if she was exactly intrusive. She'd been careful to maintain her boundaries, paying him up front for room and board, continuing to ride the bus, spending long hours at work, asking for nothing from him she couldn't repay—both to his admiration and his annoyance.

But for all of that, she still managed to bring to his life a softness, a feminine perspective and even the occasional, much-needed touch of levity that he hadn't known he was missing. She also continually surprised him, whether it was with a perceptive comment about an item in the news, a previously unsuspected devotion to M&M's—not for their chocolate content but because they shared her initials—or his current discovery that she might look like Society Princess Barbie but had a jump shot like LeBron James.

"I believe this means you're on deck to cook tonight," she said, effortlessly bouncing the ball from one slender hand to the other.

"Considering I already put dinner in the oven before we came out here, I think I'll survive," he said drily.

"For which I'm eternally grateful." Taking one quick spin, she launched the ball right through the net— again—before turning gracefully toward him. "For your continuing survival, of course." She grinned. "But also that you're in charge of the food. If we had to depend on me, we'd starve."

"No need to worry about that." He caught the ball on the rebound. "I like to cook."

"I know. And there's just something so wrong about that." She leaned contentedly against him as he looped an arm around her shoulders. "No one so brazenly male—" she pressed a kiss to his jaw as they walked back toward the house "—should be so adept in the kitchen."

He lobbed the ball toward its allotted bin in the garage, then followed her into the house. "It's not like I had a lot of choice. Growing up, it was either learn to cook or starve."

She widened her eyes in mock horror. "No takeout?"

"Not a big option with a limited budget and a lot of mouths to feed."

"No, I guess not." She was silent a moment, then said soberly, "Lilah told me you lost your mother in your teens. It must've been hard."

"No worse than yours taking off," he said easily. Seeing the faint flicker of surprise in her eyes, he found himself reaching for her. Pushing a curl that had come loose behind her ear, he let his fingers linger a moment on her soft cheek. "You've got to know that's common knowledge, Mal. It's one of the first things I ever heard about you."

"Oh, I do. It's not that. It's just… KiKi Morgan Manthauser's idea of good parenting was giving the nanny a raise. But given the way you turned out—" heading into the kitchen, she pushed back her sleeves to wash her hands, her nose crinkling appreciatively at the smell of roasting chicken "—your mom was clearly in a whole different league."

"Yeah, that's probably true. God knows, we were her whole focus. And she was good at being a parent—smart, strict, organized, but fun, with a knack for saying what you needed to hear, even though you might not think so at the time. She had a gentle, sensitive side, but she could be tough as a drill sergeant, too, the way you have to be to run a household that size. For the first fourteen years of my life, she was pretty much the sun we all revolved around."

Taking Mallory's place at the sink, he scrubbed his hands, then took the towel she handed him and dried off. "But it's been twenty years, Mal. It was tough, for a lot of different reasons, but I don't think it was as bad for me as it was for Taggart, who was closest to her, and lost without her, or even Dom, who was just old enough to decide he couldn't be hurt if he didn't let himself care about anybody again. The fact that he found Lilah, and that Taggart has Gen, is nothing short of miraculous."

"But what about you? Don't tell me that losing your mom didn't have an effect on you, too."

"Sure it did. But I was so busy looking after the younger kids, there wasn't a lot of time to dwell on it. I couldn't go my own way like Dom, or act out the way Taggart did and risk getting sent off to some tough-love military school. I had responsibilities."

"That you chose to take on," she pointed out. Having finished setting two places at the island counter, she poured them both something to drink, then seated herself as he carried their plates over and joined her.

"Yeah, but it's part of my nature." He'd come to grips with who he was a long time ago. "And it gave me the incentive to do something with my life, so I can't complain about that."

"What about your dad?"

"What about him?"

"Didn't it ever bother you that he let you take so much on your shoulders at such a young age?"

He shrugged, dismissing the old man's behavior the way he had since the day he'd turned sixteen. Flush with the success of getting his driver's license, it had been a definite downer that the first thing he'd had to do was use it to retrieve the elder Steele from a brawl at an off-base bar. But it hadn't been until later that night, as his father had gone from belligerent to maudlin to prostrate with his never-ending grief, that

Gabe had decided he'd seen enough, that for him to survive he was simply going to have to get on with the business of life.

"You do what you can," he said now. "He made his choices. I made mine. Besides, I prefer to think I'm in charge of my own destiny."

She mulled it over for a moment. "I guess, given my own less-than-sterling antecedents, I'd like to think that, too. Heaven knows, I'll never have children of my own if I don't think I can do better than my parents did. Of course, that's setting the bar really, really low." A rueful smile tipped the corners of her mouth. "Or maybe, in their case, not setting it at all."

"You'll do fine." And she would, he thought, as he glanced sideways at her sitting there with her chin propped in her hand. Out of the blue, he had a sudden vision of her, that striking face alight as she fussed over some sturdy little dark-haired boy.

Jesus. Where did that come from?

Telling himself firmly it was simply a reaction to all this talk of the past, he deliberately steered the conversation to a lighter subject. "Where'd you learn to play ball like that, anyway?"

Looking faintly relieved herself, she answered easily. "I spent every summer of my misspent youth going to camp. It was my dad's solution to not knowing what to do with me. I'm also an excellent shot with a bow and arrow and play a killer game of softball."

"Pretty impressive for the current queen of the social scene."

"Please." She flicked her fingers dismissively. "One successful fashion show hardly qualifies me as that."

It had been more than that, and they both knew it. Even without the enthusiastic write-up in that morning's paper, the verdict from participants and attendees of yesterday's exceedingly successful event had been overwhelmingly positive.

The setting, the tents, the food, the clothes and her choice of a popular radio personality to emcee the event had all gotten raves. Even Abigail Sommers, whom he'd known for years and who handed out praise as if she were being forced at gunpoint to part with a precious family jewel, had paid Mallory a number of heartfelt compliments for how impressively the show itself, and the party afterward, had gone.

"Just cross your fingers that the ball next weekend goes as smoothly," she said. "And that I'll still be able to get into my dress after the way you've been feeding me."

As far as he was concerned, she could wear what she had on and still be the most beautiful woman there. But he was always willing to do what he could to help. "If you're really worried, even though you shouldn't be, we could always burn off some calories with a little postdinner exercise."

"But the dishes—"

"Will wait." He leaned sideways, gently nipped her ear, then slid his mouth south to the crook of her neck and nuzzled her there. "I, on the other hand, am not so sure I can."

It was all that needed to be said. Sliding off the bar

stool, she came up on tiptoe and kissed him once on the mouth, then took his hand and set a course for the bedroom.

Shifting restlessly onto his side in bed later that night, Gabe spared a glance for the clock on the nightstand. The digital readout read two-forty-five.

His mouth tightened impatiently It wasn't often that he suffered from sleeplessness. He'd long ago perfected the art of switching his mind off, diving straight into dreamland and waking refreshed and ready to go five or six hours later.

So why was he lying here, spinning his wheels in the dark, tension churning in his gut?

Well, duh. The answer to that happened to be curled bonelessly beside him, her breath tickling his back, one slender arm draped trustingly around his waist.

He couldn't count the number of times in the past week he'd had lethal thoughts about Cal Morgan and what the bastard had done to Mallory. Or found himself once more hearing Mallory's distraught voice in his head saying, "I felt so stupid. I don't ever want to feel as if I'm not competent to run my own life again."

The thought of her being hurt and subsequently doubting her own worth twisted him up inside, made him want to shield and protect her, as well as assure her that from now on she had someone on her side she could depend on. Someone she could trust.

Except wasn't *trust* precisely the problem? Wasn't it the bogeyman in the room that had recently taken to stalking him, popping out at crucial moments to stab at his peace of mind?

All right. So maybe his conscience was bothering him just a little bit about certain steps he'd taken at the start of their relationship to provide Mallory with some help getting on her feet. It had seemed like the right thing to do at the time. And even now, given how well things were going for her, he couldn't honestly say he regretted it.

But he wasn't an idiot. He knew she wasn't likely to view what he'd done the same way. At least initially, until she had time to think about it, to get things in perspective and realize he'd had no choice but to take the actions he had for her own good, she was probably going to be angry.

Just the thought added to the tension twisting through him. Not that he doubted for an instant that they'd get past it, since he had no intention of accepting anything less. He might not be so far gone that he had thoughts of happily ever after—he'd learned the fallacy of that as a youngster—but he was damned if he was ready to give her up, either.

The night of the break-in he'd shocked the hell out of himself when he'd heard himself staking a claim, informing her in no uncertain terms that she was *his*. Yet the minute he'd said it, he'd known it was true. She belonged with him, at least for the foreseeable future, he thought, shifting onto his back and pulling her securely into his arms.

What's more, sometime over the past few weeks her

happiness had really begun to matter to him. More than he would've thought possible just weeks ago. And that meant he'd do whatever it took to look out for her.

Which was precisely why he wasn't going to say anything now, he thought, covering her hand with his own and pressing it to his heart. There was less than a week to go until the ball, and he was damned if he was going to risk ruining her big night just so he could get a few extra hours of sleep.

Afterward, however, they were definitely going to have to talk.

So this is what genuine accomplishment felt like, Mallory reflected, fielding yet another sincere congratulations from a passing partygoer as the Bedazzled Ball glittered its way past midnight.

It was having someone she didn't even know tell her they were having a great time.

It was looking up to see elegantly clad men and women dressed in a veritable wildflower garden of colors sitting at small, intimate tables on the balcony overhead, chatting and enjoying the spectacle of the dancing below.

It was gazing out at that very same dance floor to see a hundred plus couples dip and sway to a band she'd handpicked.

It was breathing in the sweet night air wafting through dozens of French doors thrown open to a terrace she'd transformed into a fairyland of twinkling lights and fragrant flowers.

It was having just been informed—by Nikki Volpe

of all people—that the preliminary tallies showed this year's event had raised the most money in the charity's entire history.

And it was knowing that while she'd had a hand in it all, it wouldn't feel nearly so sweet if she didn't have someone with whom to share it, she decided, as she accepted her first glass of champagne that evening from Gabe's outstretched hand.

"Thank you." Indulging herself, she took a moment to simply admire him in his faultlessly cut Armani tux. "For the drink. And for being such a good sport tonight. As busy as I've been, I noticed you took time to dance with all the elderly ladies on the board. That was really sweet of you."

He shrugged. "It was fun. Plus a number of them are long-standing Steele clients, so it was nice to have a chance to visit with them."

He wasn't fooling her for a moment. He could brush off what he'd done as self-serving, but beneath that tough guy facade, the man had a compassionate streak a mile wide.

And it just so happened that at this perfect moment in time, he was hers. Wondering if there was such a thing as being too happy, she took a sip of bubbly and gave a small, breathless laugh. "Umm. That tickles."

His eyes lighting with appreciation for her good humor, he touched his hand to her back, which was dramatically bared by the high-necked emerald gown she'd chosen for its perfect fit—and because it was the same green as his eyes. "Enjoy. You deserve a moment to savor your success." Leaning closer, he added softly for no one's ears but her own, "Just keep in mind I have plans for a private celebration when we get home."

Arching an eyebrow, she reached out and ran her fingertip over his lapel. "Do tell."

His mouth quirked. "All I'm prepared to say is that it involves a better brand of champagne and a certain pair of high heels."

Anticipation sparkled through her like the wine in her glass. "Oh, my."

"No matter what he's promising, I can do better," a different male voice promised confidently from just behind her.

"Not on your best day, little brother." With deceptive ease, Gabe took a step that effortlessly put him between Mallory and his brother Cooper.

Bemused, Mallory turned to smile at the other man, and found he'd arrived just a few steps ahead of Lilah and Dominic. The three brothers somehow wound up standing shoulder to shoulder, a sight that made her feel slightly light-headed.

Lilah came to her rescue. With a wry look on her lovely face, the blonde moved to Mallory's side, linked their arms and drew her slightly away from the men. "Breathe," she advised, her voice ripe with amusement. "I know it can be a little overwhelming the first time you find yourself face-to-face with all that unbridled testosterone, but it doesn't do to let on. As it is, none of them suffers from a lack of confidence."

Lilah was a hundred percent right. Like some recruiting poster for the tall, dark and devastating club, each man had a physical presence that came from being in top-notch shape and an ease of manner that stemmed from knowing they could handle anything that was thrown at them.

Individually, they were a sight to make any woman's pulse flutter. Together, it was a wonder they weren't hip deep in bodies from the female occupants of the room swooning at their feet.

"Just wait until the Fourth of July," Lilah advised, "when the whole family gets together to celebrate. It's always too hot for words." She fanned her face with one delicate hand. "And I'm not referring to the weather."

Unable to help herself, Mallory chuckled, thinking again that things just couldn't get any better. The ball was a success, it was beyond terrific to have a friend with such an unexpected sense of humor and the man she loved and respected desired her in return.

While it was true the two of them had yet to talk about a future, and she wasn't taking anything for granted, for the first time ever she was starting to feel as though she was making a real place for herself.

"You about ready to call it a night, sweetheart?" Stepping close to his wife, Dominic's entire demeanor turned protectively tender as he briefly touched one big hand to Lilah's cheek.

"Yes, I certainly am," she replied, with a little sigh of contentment as he reached around to knead the small of her back with one big palm. "I just need to go grab my wrap."

"I'll get it," Mallory said promptly. "As one of my last official duties of the night, I really should go make sure everything's going all right in the cloakroom."

Clearly enjoying her husband's attentions, Lilah didn't demur, just fished her ticket out of her evening purse and handed it over. "Thanks. You're a doll. We'll head in that direction and meet you."

"Okay. I'll be back in a minute," she said with a polite smile meant to include the other two men. Before she could take more than a single step away, however, Gabe tugged her close and kissed her boldly on the mouth.

"Don't be long," he said, watching with satisfaction as she blinked up at him a little dazedly before hurrying away.

Glancing around, he found he was the center of a number of pairs of interested eyes. Yet it was only the reactions of the three people closest to him that he gave a damn about.

Lilah's expression reflected warm approval. She'd clearly taken to Mallory and it was obvious the two of them were becoming genuine friends.

Dom's reaction, though more guarded, also seemed to be positive, as well as a little smug, no great surprise since he'd had a hell of a good time in Belgrade needling Gabe by murmuring, "the bigger they are, the harder they fall" under his breath at the most inappropriate times.

Only Cooper appeared to have some reservations. Not that anyone who didn't know him like a brother would notice—the smile he sent Gabe was totally pleasant. But Gabe saw the shadow of concern in his eyes just the same.

He wasn't in the mood to worry about it tonight, however. So it was just as well that Dom slapped the younger man on the shoulder and said, "Come on, kid. Do me a favor and hunt down a valet to bring the car around, will you? That will give me a sporting chance to get my lovely bride to the door without every woman in sight trotting up to share her labor and delivery story." He gave a slight shudder. "Trust me. Some of the stuff is scarier than trying to evade a sniper while picking your way blindfolded through a minefield."

Family, Gabe thought minutes later, as he watched the members of his get swallowed up by the crowd. As crazy as they sometimes made him, he couldn't imagine his life without them. For exactly that reason it had been good for them to see him with Mallory, he reflected, to let them see for themselves that she was currently an important part of his life.

"There you are, dear." Separating themselves from an elderly trio of friends, sisters Eleanor and Annalise DeMarco, longtime Steele clients, permanent Bedazzled board members, and both spry and sharp as tacks—although they'd long passed their eightieth birthdays—approached. "Alone at last, you handsome young devil."

Smiling, Gabe held up a hand in surrender. "I'm not sure I can handle another dance, Anna, if that's what you came for," he said to the older, more effusive of the two, who was resplendent tonight in diamonds and pale blue silk that closely resembled the shade of her hair. "You wore me out the first time around."

"Oh, you!" she said, her faded brown eyes twinkling. "That was nothing. If I were forty years younger—"

"Hmph," Eleanor, tall and angular and wearing mauve and rubies, interjected tartly. "More like fifty."

"I swear I'd put you through your paces somewhere other than the dance floor," her sister said, giving Gabe a naughty wink.

"She always was a trollop," Eleanor said with sniff a of disapproval, throwing a long-suffering gaze his way.

Amused as he always was by their bickering, Gabe let them go on for a few more minutes before he finally intervened. "Ladies, you know I'm always glad to see you, but as it happens I was just on my way to find Mallory."

"Who is precisely the reason we came to talk to you," Eleanor said, abruptly perking up.

"Yes, she most certainly is," Annalise agreed with an actual nod of approval at her sister.

"You know, of course, that we were a little dubious when we first agreed to take her on. There was all that unpleasantness with her father—"

"Odious man," Anna remarked.

"—and despite the time she'd spent as a Bedazzled volunteer over the years, she did have a rather flighty reputation."

"Clearly exaggerated, we can see now."

"But whatever her difficulties in the past, she's come nicely up to the mark now and we just wanted to let you know how truly grateful we are that you brought her to our attention," Eleanor said firmly. "Even without your extremely generous pledge, this year's event has been the most successful ever—"

"No doubt in part due to the wonderful fashion event your young lady put together."

"—and we couldn't be more pleased with her performance. Now, don't worry—"

"No, no, we wouldn't want you to do that," Anna said.

"Sister and I will continue to honor your request for anonymity. But we thought you'd like to know that we board members have been talking amongst ourselves tonight and have decided to ask her to stay on for next year. We really can't thank you enough for twisting our arms and insisting we give her a try."

He couldn't contain a smile as he imagined Mallory's elation when she learned the good news. "I just gave things a nudge in the right direction. The credit is all Mallory's."

"Apparently not," said a cool, achingly familiar voice.

His heart dropped to his shoes and he slowly turned, almost afraid of what he would find.

For good reason as it turned out.

Because Mallory stood not a foot away, staring at him as if he were a stranger, a shattered look in her eyes.

Ten

"Dammit, don't look at me that way," Gabe said fiercely.

Swallowing hard, Mallory said nothing. No matter what, she assured herself as he pulled her with an inescapable grip into the first deserted meeting room they came across outside the hotel ballroom, she was not going to break down.

Not when she'd managed to keep a firm grasp on her composure while Anna and Eleanor DeMarco had fussed over her, smiling and patting her shoulder as they'd reiterated what she'd already heard them tell Gabe.

How the ball was a smashing success. How exceedingly pleased everyone on the board was with what she'd managed to achieve in such a short time. And how, in light of her impressive performance, the board had agreed that the coordinator's job was hers for the upcoming year if she wanted it.

It had been her moment of triumph, the fulfillment of what only six weeks earlier had seemed like an unattainable dream.

So she'd smiled and nodded, said *thank you very much* and *yes, please*, acting thrilled in a truly Oscar worthy performance.

And all the while her mind had been riveted on what the sisters so very discreetly had *not* seen fit to say.

That she owed her success to Gabriel who had promised a large amount of money to the charity in order to secure her present position for her.

The knife that seemed to be jammed in her heart twisted a little harder at the reminder.

Somehow she'd gotten through the exchange with the sisters without losing her aplomb. Just as she'd managed not to succumb to the tremors that had threatened to overtake her when Gabe had encircled her wrist with his hard fingers before she could bolt.

She hadn't let loose with the furious denial that had crowded her throat when he'd declared, face grim, "We need to talk." Much less dug in her heels and shrilly refused to budge when he'd hustled her out of the room like some fugitive he was determined not to let escape.

No. Her effort to be viewed as someone other than the despicable Cal Morgan's useless daughter was far too new, and her quest to be taken seriously still too important to her, to jeopardize either by making a scene.

But there was nobody watching now.

"Just how should I look at you, Gabriel? Why don't you tell me?" Feeling his touch like a brand to her soul, she tugged at her wrist, profoundly relieved when he let her go. "Should I simper with gratitude because you bought me my job?"

Stepping back out of reach, she saw a nerve jump in his jaw, and the small seed of hope that she may have gotten it wrong withered inside her.

"Or wait, maybe I'm supposed to gaze at you with admiration for the way you duped me into actually believing you respected me."

"I *do* respect you," he said forcefully.

"Oh, please!" Turning away, she fought to hide the pain that was starting to radiate through her like cracks spidering across a shattered windowpane. "Don't insult us both! I told you I could take care of myself. And you went behind my back anyway! You manipulated me, dammit!"

"No." Catching her by the shoulder, he swung her around. "I merely provided you with an opportunity— and look how well you did with it!"

She knocked his hand away, filled with increasing sadness and frustration as he refused to see reason. "But don't you see? It was an opportunity I couldn't secure on my own!"

"So? What does that matter when you weigh it against everything else? I mean, honestly, are you going to stand there and tell me that if you'd known I was involved, you'd have passed up the job to flip burgers someplace?"

"That's not the point!"

"The hell it isn't." Untying his bow tie with a jerk, he heedlessly yanked the top few studs free on his shirt, his face growing more and more shuttered. "All I did was get your foot in the door, Mal. You did the rest."

"Okay, Gabriel. Let's say you're right. If, as you just so arrogantly pointed out, I couldn't afford to turn down the position, then why bother to lie about it? I'll tell you why. Because you knew all along that going behind my back was wrong!"

"Jesus!" He raked a hand impatiently through his dark hair. "Do you think, just for a minute, you could try to be rational here? The truth of the matter is I tried being up-front with you, but you wouldn't have it. So what was I supposed to do? Turn my back, walk away, leave you to starve in that ratty little garret where you were already three months late on the damn rent?"

"How on earth do you know I was... Oh, my God." She raised a suddenly shaking hand to her chest as she stared at him in horror. "Oh, my God. I should've known it was too good to be true. There never was a cousin Ivan, was there? It was you. It was you all along."

His sudden stillness spoke volumes and then he exploded into motion. "You're right!" Pacing away, he whirled to look her square in the face. "I arranged for you to get that money. Just like I arranged for you to get the job. But no matter what you want to believe, it was never about me trying to control you. What I will agree, is that I should've told you—and I should've done it long before now."

"So why didn't you!"

"Because, again, I was trying to look out for your best interests. Once I got to know you and we started to feel this…connection…I knew what I'd done wasn't going to be easy for you to accept. So I decided to wait, rather than risk ruining tonight for you."

In that instant, with her world crumbling around her, she lost the desperate grip she had on her temper. "Would you listen to yourself? *You* knew, *you* decided. *You* thought it would be best to spare me the hardship of the truth." Sick with betrayal, she finally lashed out. "Gosh, Gabe—how very Cal Morgan of you!"

His face went white.

And just like that, her anger vanished, washed away by a profound grief for what she'd believed they had— and what she'd just lost. Yet she still had a spark of pride and she'd rather die than admit to him that her heart was breaking.

"Whatever connection we did or didn't have, it's over. I don't want to see you. I don't want to hear from you. What I *do* want is for you to leave me alone. Do you hear me, Gabriel? Please. Just leave me the hell alone."

Then no longer caring what anyone else might think, she turned and wrenched open the door, picked up the full skirt of her gown and fled down the corridor. She sped across the lobby, dashed out under the portico and along the curving sidewalk, her only thought to put as much distance between them as she could manage.

She was halfway down the street when it dawned on her she didn't have her purse.

Not that it mattered, she realized a little hysterically, slowing as she fought to catch her breath. What good would it do her? The ten dollars she'd tucked inside it would barely begin to cover the cost of a cab ride to Gabe's. And even if she used it for the bus, between transfers and the reduced nighttime schedule it would take her well over an hour to get out to his place.

Where Gabriel would no doubt be waiting for her. And even if somehow by the grace of God he wasn't, what then? Did she pack a bag, call a cab, go to a hotel where with his resources he'd have no trouble tracking her down if he chose?

And why should she believe Mr. Master-of-every-one-else's-universe wouldn't do precisely that? She'd have to be crazy to think he'd leave her alone simply because she'd asked.

But where else could she go? What other choices did she have?

God help her, she didn't know—she couldn't think. The only thing that seemed clear was that she couldn't stay here, she thought, stumbling a little as she resumed her pell-mell pace and the first tears began to track down her face.

By the time a gleaming white limo with darkly tinted windows swept past her moments later, she was a mess.

She'd cried her mascara into rivulets down her cheeks, her hair was coming down and her feet, which she'd bared rather than risk breaking her neck in her high heels, were bruised and filthy.

God. Could this night get any worse?

Up ahead, the limo abruptly veered toward the curb, stopped, then slowly reversed. Her heart began to pound and she picked up her skirts to run—until a rear window glided down and she recognized the occupant.

When the door promptly swung open seconds later and the figure beckoned her with an autocratic crook of a hand, she only hesitated a second. Then with a sob of relief she crossed the sidewalk and climbed in.

Seconds later, the vehicle rolled away and disappeared into the inky Denver night.

Eleven

Gabe knew instinctively from the insistent peal of the doorbell that whoever was pushing the ringer wasn't Mallory.

Yet apparently his heart wasn't as certain as his head or he wouldn't feel such a crushing mix of disappointment and despair when he strode down his front hall, yanked open the door and found Cooper standing there.

For a second it was almost more than he could bear.

Then he got a grip, reminding himself that he'd brought this on himself. And that he'd get through it since the only other alternative was giving up—and that was no option at all. Still, with the exception of his unfulfilled longing for one special woman, he was no more in the mood for company now than he had been for the past six days.

Erasing all expression from his face, he considered his brother. "What're you doing here?"

"I came by to give you a report on the Landow search."

"Have we found him yet?"

"No."

"Okay." He inclined his head a fraction. "Thanks for the update." Giving the door a firm shove, he turned away.

"Aw, hell." In a move Cooper never could've pulled off if Gabe had been anywhere near the top of his game, the younger man shot his foot into the rapidly dwindling gap, slapped his hand against the glossy wood panel and shoved, blowing past him into the house. "That wasn't exactly the truth," he said, prudently backing out of reach a few feet down the hallway. "The real reason I'm here is that everyone's worried about you."

For maybe half a second, Gabe considered teaching his brother a lesson about the consequences of shoving in where you weren't wanted. In the next instant, the irony of the thought struck him, and his mouth twisted. Jesus. After the way he'd screwed things up with Mallory—

Reining in his emotions, he closed the door. "Everybody being…?"

For the first time Coop looked faintly apologetic. "Well, all of us guys…but mainly Lilah and Gen."

"And what? You drew the short straw?"

"Something like that."

It figured. The last time one of his brothers' wives

had gotten worried, he'd been the one in Cooper's place—and wound up taking a roundhouse to the face from Taggart for his trouble.

"Goddammit," he said but without any heat, padding past Cooper as he headed down the hall. "You've got five minutes to say or do whatever you have to so you can go back and convince the girls I'm fine and they need to just leave this alone."

"Yeah, well…" Trailing behind, Cooper followed him into the family room. His sharp gaze skimmed the pillow and blanket piled on the floor, the dishes sitting across the way in the sink and the newspapers littering the bar, before coming back to Gabe's face. "I don't know," he said dubiously. "You're looking a little rough around the edges here, bro."

He ran a hand over his unshaven cheek, glanced down at his denim-clad legs, then shrugged. "So I'm taking a few days off. Big deal. I'm allowed."

"Well, sure, but…" Walking into the kitchen, Cooper poured himself a cup of hours-old coffee, took a sip, then grimaced. "You want to talk about it?" he said quietly, dumping the contents of the mug into the sink.

When Gabe just looked at him, Cooper sighed. "Look, Deke says when he ran into you at Jilly's Java Sunday morning you were still in your tux and looking pretty grim. And Dom says Mallory sent word to Lilah that same afternoon that she was going to be un-reachable for a while but would be looking for a new place to live. Which Lilah admits she passed on to you.

Then you don't come into work… Come on, Gabe. A two-year-old with one of those big fat crayons could complete this picture."

Gabe felt a muscle jump in his cheek. Most of the time he genuinely liked his family. Then there were moments like this when they made him feel as hemmed in as a tiger stuffed into a cat carrier.

Still, there didn't seem to be any way out of the conversation but to be honest. "Okay. So we had a fight. We'll work it out." Or so he hoped with every inch of his being.

"Is there anything I can do?"

"Except give me some space? No." Hell, there was nothing *he* could do—despite the fact that sitting on his hands was taking an ever-increasing toll with each day, each hour, each minute that passed.

But that didn't change the hard truth—that whatever happened next was up to Mallory.

Of course, that wasn't how he'd felt Saturday night, he reflected.

He still wasn't sure how long he'd stood in that meeting room, cut to the bone that she would ever compare him to her father. At the same time his gut had screamed at him to go after her, chase her down, *make* her listen to reason.

Eventually, his sanity—or so he'd considered it at the time—had prevailed. Deciding they both needed some space to cool off, he'd made his way to the hotel bar where he'd nursed a scotch and asked himself why he was surprised by what had just happened. Hadn't he predicted she'd overreact exactly the way she had? Wasn't that precisely why he'd held off telling her in the first place?

Hell, yes. But she was an intelligent woman, and once she calmed down and realized she was being unreasonable, he'd been confident they'd get past that particular bump in the road.

That line of thinking had sustained him all the way home. And though he'd felt a distinct uneasiness when he'd crossed the threshold and realized there was nobody there but him, he'd shrugged it off, as well, figuring one of her coworkers had seen her distress at the hotel and taken her in for the night.

By dawn, when he'd gone out to get coffee and run into Deke, he'd been starting to feel less sanguine. And as the morning had progressed without any word from her, he'd found himself wandering restlessly through his too-quiet house, seeing little traces of her everywhere—in the trio of lacy panties folded next to his socks in the laundry room, the book she'd left on the nightstand next to the bed, the bouquet of daisies on the kitchen table.

And he'd started to wonder: What if she'd actually meant it when she said she never wanted to see him again?

But that simply wasn't acceptable. He was a man who made things happen and he wasn't ready for their relationship to end. Hell, they were just getting started.

Still, like a fatal crack in a faulty foundation, with that first doubt he'd felt something inside him shift.

Then while he'd still been attempting to cobble things back together, Lilah had called to tell him Mallory was safe and that he shouldn't worry.

Then she'd quietly added she was sorry and hung up.

And standing there in his kitchen clutching his silent phone, he'd realized that was it. There hadn't been a word about Mallory returning. Not a hint where she was. No message for him at all.

Still like a sharp stick in the eye, he'd gotten the point. *We're through and I'm not coming back.*

Desolation had slammed into him, nearly taking him out at the knees. Sliding onto a bar stool, he'd dimly realized that despite what he'd told Mallory a couple of weeks ago, the only other time he'd felt this sort of pain had been nearly two decades earlier. That was the day he'd finally accepted that while the father he'd worshipped was still breathing and walking around, inside his dad was as dead as the woman they'd buried nearly two years before.

Yet that couldn't be right, Gabe had thought, the crack in the bedrock of what he believed about himself widening into a crevasse. Because he'd loved his father with all a firstborn son's fervor, while his feelings for Mallory…

Sweet Jesus. The truth had blown through him like a howitzer blast, practically knocking him off the stool.

Because the truth was he'd been pretty much a goner the first time he'd seen her at that very first party all those years ago.

Reeling, all he'd been able to think was that he had to find her. That no matter what it took, he had to track her down and tell her how he felt. That she had a right to know his heart before she made any decisions about their future.

He'd climbed to his feet, scooped up his keys—only to falter as the last thing she'd said to him had suddenly sounded in his head as clearly as if she'd actually been in the room.

I don't want to see you. I don't want to hear from you. What I want is for you to leave me alone.

And that's when it had dawned on him that if he was ever to have a hope of regaining her trust, he had to back off. That he had to give her space and trust her to make her own decision about their future.

So that's what he was doing, even though the waiting was killing him.

"Listen," he said, plucking the cup out of Cooper's hand and herding him out of the kitchen and back down the hall. "I'll be fine. When have you ever known me not to be? I just need some time to myself for a change. Tell everyone I'm taking a little vacation. God knows I'm overdue."

"Well, yeah, that's true." Despite his agreement and the fact that he was allowing Gabe to ease him out the door, Cooper's gaze was still troubled. "Just—take care of yourself, all right?"

"You got it," Gabe replied. Standing at the door, he watched for a moment as his brother got into his red SUV, pulled out of the drive and sped off down the street, passing a white limo coming the other way.

Then he turned around and went back inside. To wait.

* * *

Mallory glanced out the limousine window for the hundredth time.

"Good grief, my dear, quit looking so nervous," Abigail Anson Sommers said tartly. "As I've already told you, there's no need to rush into this. You're welcome to stay at Cedar Hill as long as you'd like."

"I know. And I appreciate your offer more than I can say," she said, turning back to the elegant old lady. "But I need to do this. I need to try, at least."

Because Abigail's offer notwithstanding, she really *didn't* have another choice, she thought as the limo slowed for the final turn into Gabriel's driveway and her already jittery stomach bounced up into her throat.

Not if she was going to have a hope of getting on with her life.

For nearly a week now she'd waited for Gabriel, expecting him to marshal all his impressive resources, do whatever it took to track her down so he could tell her, in his big, bold, take-charge kind of way, that he didn't intend to let her walk away.

Only he hadn't shown up.

Not the first couple of days, when she'd been so angry and hurt that she'd easily used up a lifetime allotment of curses and tears.

Not during the next two days, either, when her emotions had finally settled enough for her to get some perspective on what had happened between them, forcing her to face some hard truths. Not only about Gabe but about herself, as well.

And heaven knew, there'd been no sign of him in the past forty-eight hours, as she'd grown more and more restless and impatient while wondering what on earth was keeping him.

The woman she'd been three months ago would have concluded his absence meant he didn't care. But the woman she was now—who through recent trials and accomplishments was stronger, steadier, possessed of some genuine, hard-won confidence and a growing sense of self-worth—refused to believe it.

And that was the Mallory who'd awakened this morning to a startling thought. What if Gabriel had actually taken her angry, overwrought, parting shots to heart? What if all this time he'd stayed away because that's what she'd told him she wanted?

At first she'd blown it off, telling herself not to be ridiculous. People said things they didn't mean in the heat of an argument all the time. As savvy as he was— and as secure in his masculinity—certainly after the past few weeks he had to know she cared about him.

Except… She'd never actually told him. Not straight-out. And the more she'd thought about it, the clearer it had become that as much as she missed him, and despite the sharp little thorn of insecurity his failure to appear had lodged near her heart, she'd *needed* this time.

She'd needed it to examine how she felt. Needed it to decide just what it was that she wanted.

"Well if you feel so strongly, then obviously you must see this through," Abigail said briskly, reaching over to give Mallory's hand a quick squeeze as the limo purred to a stop. "Just one further piece of advice, child. Don't try. *Do*."

Oh my. Was it her imagination or had Lilah's elegant, autocratic, octogenarian grandmother just channeled Yoda?

Unbidden, a spurt of laughter squeezed past the lump in Mallory's throat and impulsively she leaned over to press a kiss to Abigail's paper-thin cheek.

"Thank you, Mrs. Sommers. For everything. I don't know what I would have done without you. If you hadn't rescued me off the street and taken me home with you…" She paused to steady her voice. "I'll never be able to repay you."

"Oh bosh!" Abigail said brusquely.

As the chauffeur opened the door, she shooed Mallory away. But not before Mallory saw the hint of moisture sheening the older woman's eyes.

"Good heavens, Clarence," Abigail went on imperiously, addressing her grizzled employee, "this younger generation is appallingly sentimental, don't you agree?"

"Yes, madam," he said solemnly, giving Mallory a wink before handing her out of the car and escorting her to the front door. "You'll do fine, miss," he said, tipping his cap.

Then the limo backed out of the drive, and impulsively trying the knob, she found to her surprise that the door was unlocked.

So after one more deep, steadying breath, she walked inside.

She found Gabe standing at the tall windows at the back of the house. He was gazing moodily out at his big backyard, looking quite unlike his usual elegant self, dressed as he was in a faded black T-shirt and ancient jeans, with his hair mussed, his feet bare and what looked to be several days' worth of black stubble shadowing his face.

As if only then registering her footsteps, he started to turn. "Dammit, Coop, what could you possibly—" The words died on his lips. "Mallory. You're here."

"Yes. Yes I am."

For an instant his eyes squeezed shut and then he took a swift step toward her and her heart lifted—only to plummet again as he jerked to a stop and his expression closed up.

All right, she thought, trying to control her hammering pulse. For a moment she'd hoped this was going to be easy, that they would simply fall into each other's arms and kiss and talk and everything would instantly be all right again…

Except she'd learned real life didn't quite work that way. Sometimes, no matter how frightened or unsure or how big the risk, you just had to lay your heart on the line and hope for the best.

She breathed in, breathed out. Cleared her throat and plunged in. "There are some things I need to say."

Thrusting his hands in his front pockets, he inclined his head. "Okay."

Eyeing the rigid set of his shoulders, she began slowly, "We both said some pretty hard things the other night, and I'm not going to apologize for most of them. But I do regret one thing. You are everything my father isn't. You're strong and dependable and honorable and a man to be counted on—and if I made you think for a minute that I didn't believe that with ever fiber of my being, I'm sorrier than I can say."

Taking a breath, she again tried to gauge his reaction, her stomach tightening even more as he simply stood there, not giving away a clue as to what he was thinking. "Don't get me wrong. I still don't agree with the way you did things." Her heart gave a little lurch as the line of his mouth grew even more forbidding. "But I know you truly thought you were looking out for me. Your methods may have been high-handed, but your intentions were pure. And that means a lot."

She swallowed. "I guess what I'm trying to say—" she dredged up a slight, tentative smile, still praying fruitlessly for a glimmer of response in return "—is that I love you, Gabe. I know I've made my own share of mistakes, but if you'd be interested in giving us another chance—"

Before she even finished what she had to say, he was across the room. Hauling her into his arms, he demolished every last inch of space between them.

The joy—the relief—was so intense that for a while it was all she could do to absorb it. Eventually, however, she realized the thumping she felt was the furious beat of his heart and the last of the coiled tension that had been strangling her the past hours abruptly unwound.

Oh, no, not indifferent, she thought, holding him

fiercely as he rocked her against him, his face buried in her hair.

Not indifferent by a long shot.

"God but you gave me a scare," he said finally. Loosening his hold on her, he brought up his hands to cradle her face as he rested his forehead against hers. "Walking in here, looking so damn serious and beautiful. I thought—"

His throat worked, and the sight of him—big, strong, and normally so articulate—struggling to find his voice made her own throat ache.

"I thought you'd come to say goodbye. Before I ever got the chance to tell you how sorry I am for hurting you. Or admit what a fool I've been. The truth is, there's a lot I need to tell you—some of it about the past and my feelings for my dad that I'm only starting to see myself. But for now that can wait."

He leaned back just a little more, exposing all the naked emotion on that compelling face. His eyes, green and clear, met hers directly and this time he wasn't holding anything back. "What won't wait is this—I love you, Mallory. Looking back, I was pretty much a goner from the first time we met, only I was too stubborn to see it then." His strong, sensuous mouth quirked a bare fraction. "I was convinced I didn't want that kind of complication in my life, and I think I would've gone right on believing it if I hadn't walked into Annabelle's that day.

"But seeing you there, all alone, knowing you were in trouble… As much as I wanted to, I just couldn't walk away—not and live with myself. And you know what?"

She shook her head, pretty sure she was staring up at him with her heart in her eyes—and knowing she'd never find anyone else who would cherish her more.

"It was the best decision I ever made. And if you'll give me the chance, I swear I'll spend the rest of forever making sure you feel the same way."

His lips found hers then. And standing there, with the sunshine pouring in through the window around them, Mallory knew that with Gabriel Steele she'd always be safe.

* * * * *

Happily ever after is just the beginning…

*Turn the page for a sneak preview of
DANCING ON SUNDAY AFTERNOONS
by
Linda Cardillo*

*Harlequin Everlasting—Every great love
has a story to tell. ™
A brand-new line from Harlequin Books
launching this February!*

Prologue

Giulia D'Orazio
1983

I had two husbands—Paolo and Salvatore.

Salvatore and I were married for thirty-two years. I still live in the house he bought for us; I still sleep in our bed. All around me are the signs of our life together. My bedroom window looks out over the garden he planted. In the middle of the city, he coaxed tomatoes, peppers, zucchini—even grapes for his wine—out of the ground. On weekends, he used to drive up to his cousin's farm in Waterbury and bring back manure. In the winter, he wrapped the peach tree and the fig tree with rags and black rubber hoses against the cold, his massive, coarse hands gentling those trees as if they were his fragile-skinned babies. My neighbor, Dominic Grazza, does that for me now. My boys have no time for the garden.

In the front of the house, Salvatore planted roses. The roses I take care of myself. They are giant, cream-colored, fragrant. In the afternoons, I like to sit out on the porch with my coffee, protected from the eyes of the neighborhood by that curtain of flowers.

Salvatore died in this house thirty-five years ago. In the last months, he lay on the sofa in the parlor so he could be in the middle of everything. Except for the two oldest boys, all the children were still at home and we ate together every evening. Salvatore could see the dining room table from the sofa, and he could hear everything that was said. "I'm not dead, yet," he told me. "I want to know what's going on."

When my first grandchild, Cara, was born, we brought her to him, and he held her on his chest, stroking her tiny head. Sometimes they fell asleep together.

Over on the radiator cover in the corner of the parlor is the portrait Salvatore and I had taken on our twenty-fifth anniversary. This brooch I'm wearing today, with the diamonds—I'm wearing it in the photograph also—Salvatore gave it to me that day. Upstairs on my dresser is a jewelry box filled with necklaces and bracelets and earrings. All from Salvatore.

I am surrounded by the things Salvatore gave me,

or did for me. But, God forgive me, as I lie alone now in my bed, it is Paolo I remember.

Paolo left me nothing. Nothing, that is, that my family, especially my sisters, thought had any value. No house. No diamonds. Not even a photograph.

But after he was gone, and I could catch my breath from the pain, I knew that I still had something. In the middle of the night, I sat alone and held them in my hands, reading the words over and over until I heard his voice in my head. I had Paolo's letters.

* * * * *

This February...

Catch NASCAR Superstar **Carl Edwards** *in*
SPEED DATING!

Kendall assesses risk for a living—
so she's the last person you'd
expect to see on the arm of a
race-car driver who thrives on the
unpredictable. But when a bizarre
turn of events—and NASCAR
hotshot Dylan Hargreave—inspire
her to trade in her ever-so-structured
existence for "life in the fast lane"
she starts to feel she might be
on to something!

REQUEST YOUR FREE BOOKS!

2 FREE NOVELS PLUS 2 FREE GIFTS!

Passionate, Powerful, Provocative!

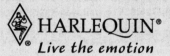

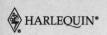

EVERLASTING LOVE™

Every great love has a story to tell™

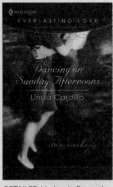

Save $1.⁰⁰ off

the purchase of
any Harlequin
Everlasting Love novel

Coupon valid from January 1, 2007
until April 30, 2007.

Valid at retail outlets in the U.S. only.
Limit one coupon per customer.

5 65373 00076 2   (8100)0 11302

HEUSCPN0407

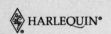

EVERLASTING LOVE™

Every great love has a story to tell™

Save $1.00 off

the purchase of
any Harlequin
Everlasting Love novel

Coupon valid from January 1, 2007
until April 30, 2007.

Valid at retail outlets in Canada only.
Limit one coupon per customer.

52607370

HECDNCPN0407

What a month!

In February watch for

Rancher and Protector
Part of the Western Weddings miniseries
BY JUDY CHRISTENBERRY

The Boss's Pregnancy Proposal
BY RAYE MORGAN

Also in February, expect
MORE of what you love
as the Harlequin Romance line
increases to six titles per month.

Silhouette® Desire

Don't miss the first book
in THE ROYALS trilogy:

THE FORBIDDEN PRINCESS
(SD #1780)

by national bestselling author

DAY LECLAIRE

Moments before her loveless royal wedding,
Princess Alyssa was kidnapped by a mysterious man
who'd do anything to stop the ceremony. Even if that
meant marrying the forbidden princess himself!

On sale February 2007 from Silhouette Desire!

THE ROYALS
Stories of scandals and secrets
amidst the most powerful palaces.

Make sure to read the other titles in the series:
THE PRINCE'S MISTRESS
On sale March 2007
THE ROYAL WEDDING NIGHT
On sale April 2007

*Available wherever books are sold, including most
bookstores, supermarkets, discount stores and drugstores.*